Praise for NIGHTBIRD

A *New York Times Book Review* Editors' Choice

"Hoffman reminds us that there are secrets everywhere, and in these moments of unexpected discovery, *Nightbird* soars." —*The New York Times Book Review*

★ "Alice Hoffman has a gift for melding magic and realism in a way that makes nearly anything seem possible." —*Shelf Awareness*, Starred

"The mix of romance and magic is irresistible and the tension, compelling. . . . Enchanting." —*Kirkus Reviews*

"The tone, mystical but not too dark, makes this a good choice for readers who want to imagine just a bit of magic in their lives." —*The Horn Book Magazine*

"The book's evocative setting and distinctive characters will immediately hook readers, and the history of Twig's family, uncovered bit by bit, will keep them engaged." —*Publishers Weekly*

"Spare, evocative prose makes Twig's loneliness palpable, and the savvy revelation of details will have readers gasping." —*The Bulletin of the Center for Children's Books*

"This novel is a recipe for a page-turning plot." —*VOYA*

"A clever narrator, beautiful imagery, and [a] quirky cast of secondary characters." —*School Library Journal*

"Bestselling Hoffman offers a quiet, gentle fantasy where crossroads and moonlight have magical uses, and friendship and determination can heal centuries-old wounds." —*Booklist*

"*Nightbird* is like reentering a wonderful dream that you vaguely remember." —Lois Lowry, two-time Newbery Medal–winning author of *The Giver*

"Alice Hoffman is pretty much my favorite living author, and *Nightbird* is just one more reason why. Every book she writes is a treasured gift for her readers." —Charles de Lint, author of *Moonheart* and the Wildlings series

"I loved *Nightbird*. Past and present unite to solve a magically intriguing problem of witches, feathers, and owls." —Penelope Lively, winner of the Carnegie Medal and the Booker Prize

Nightbird

ALICE HOFFMAN

A YEARLING BOOK

Text copyright © 2015 by Alice Hoffman
Cover art copyright © 2016 by Erin McGuire

All rights reserved. Published in the United States by Yearling, an imprint of Random House Children's Books, a division of Penguin Random House LLC, New York. Originally published in hardcover in the United States by Wendy Lamb Books, an imprint of Random House Children's Books, New York, in 2015.

Yearling and the jumping horse design are registered trademarks of Penguin Random House LLC.

Visit us on the Web! randomhousekids.com

Educators and librarians, for a variety of teaching tools, visit us at RHTeachersLibrarians.com

The Library of Congress has cataloged the hardcover edition of this work as follows:
Hoffman, Alice.
Nightbird / Alice Hoffman. — First edition.
pages cm
ISBN 978-0-385-38958-7 (trade) — ISBN 978-0-385-38959-4 (lib. bdg.) —
ISBN 978-0-385-38960-0 (ebook) — ISBN 978-0-385-38961-7 (pbk.)
[1. Blessing and cursing—Fiction. 2. Witchcraft—Fiction.
3. Interpersonal relations—Fiction. 4. Wings (Anatomy)—Fiction.
5. Family life—Massachusetts—Fiction. 6. Community life—Massachusetts—Fiction.
7. Massachusetts—Fiction.] I. Title.
PZ7.H67445Nig 2015
[Fic]—dc23
2013043838

Printed in the United States of America

10 9 8 7 6 5 4 3 2 1

First Yearling Edition 2016

Random House Children's Books supports the First Amendment and celebrates the right to read.

CONTENTS

CHAPTER ONE

The Way It Began

YOU CAN'T BELIEVE EVERYTHING YOU HEAR, not even in Sidwell, Massachusetts, where every person is said to tell the truth and the apples are so sweet people come from as far as New York City during the apple festival. There are rumors that a mysterious creature lives in our town. Some people insist it's a bird bigger than an eagle; others say it's a dragon, or an oversized bat that resembles a person. Certainly this being, human or animal or something in between, exists nowhere else in this world. Children whisper that we have a monster in our midst, half man, half myth, and that fairy tales are real in

1

Berkshire County. At the Sidwell General Store and at the gas station tourists can buy T-shirts decorated with a red-eyed winged beast with VISIT SIDWELL printed underneath.

Every time I see one of these shirts in a shop, I casually drop it into the garbage bin.

In my opinion, people should be careful about the stories they tell.

All the same, whenever things go missing the monster is blamed. Weekends are the worst times for these odd thefts. Bread deliveries to the Starline Diner are several loaves short of the regular order. Clothes hanging on the line vanish. I know there's no such thing as a monster, but the thief has struck my family, as a matter of fact. One minute there were four pies sitting out on the kitchen counter to cool, and the next minute the back door was left open and one of the pies was missing. An old quilt left out on our porch disappeared one Saturday. There were no footprints on our lawn, but I did have a prickle of fear when I stood at the back door that morning, gazing into the woods. I thought I spied a solitary figure running through a thicket of trees, but it might have only been mist, rising from the ground.

No one knows who takes these things, whether pranks are being played, or someone—or something—is truly in need, or if it is the creature that everyone assumes lives within the borders of our town. People in Sidwell argue as much as people do anywhere, but everyone agrees on one thing: Our monster can only be seen at night, and then only if you are standing at your window, or walking on a lane near the orchards, or if you happen to be passing our house.

We live on Old Mountain Road, in a farmhouse that is over two hundred years old, with nooks and crannies and three brick fireplaces, all big enough for me to stand in, even though I am tall for twelve. From our front door there's a sweeping view of the woods that contain some of the oldest trees in Massachusetts. Behind us are twenty acres of apple orchards. We grow a special variety called Pink. One of my ancestors planted the first Pink apple tree in Sidwell. Some people say Johnny Appleseed himself, who introduced apple trees all over our country, presented our family with a one-of-a-kind seedling when he wandered through town on his way out west. We make Pink applesauce, Pink apple cake, and two shades of Pink apple pie, light and dark. In the summer, before we have apples, we have Pink peach berry pie, and in the late spring there is Hot-Pink strawberry rhubarb pie, made from fruit grown in the garden behind our house. Rhubarb looks like red celery; it's bitter, but when combined with strawberries it's delicious. I like the idea of something bitter and something sweet mixed together to create something incredible. Maybe that's because I come from a family in which we don't expect each other to be like anyone else. Being unusual is not unusual for the Fowlers.

My mother's piecrust is said to be the finest in New England and our Pink cider is famous all over Massachusetts. People come from as far away as Cambridge and Lowell just to try them. We bring most of our pies and cupcakes to be sold at the General Store that's run by Mr. Stern, who can sell as many as my mother can bake. I've always wished that I was more like her instead of my awkward, gawky self. As a girl my mother attended ballet lessons at Miss Ellery's Dance School in town, and she's still graceful, even when she's picking apples or hauling baskets of fruit across the lawn. But my arms and legs are too long, and I tend to stumble over my own feet. The only thing I'm good at is running. And keeping secrets. I'm excellent at that. I've had a lot of practice.

My mother has honey-colored hair that she pins up with a silver clip whenever she bakes. My hair is dark;

sometimes I don't even know what color it is, a sort of blackish brown, the color of tree bark, or a night that has no stars. It gets so tangled while I'm out in the woods that this year I cut it out of frustration, just hacked at it with a pair of nail scissors, and now it is worse than ever, even though my mother says I look like a pixie. Looking like a pixie was not what I was after. I wanted to look like my mother, who everyone says was the prettiest girl in town when she was my age, and now is the most beautiful woman in the entire county.

But she's also terribly sad. If my mother smiles it's something of a miracle, that's how rare it is. People in town are always kind to her, but they whisper about her, and refer to her as "poor Sophie Fowler." We aren't poor, though my mother has worked hard since her parents passed away and she came back to take over the orchard. All the same, I know why people feel sorry for her. I feel sorry for her, too. Despite the fact that my mother grew up in this town, she's always alone. In the evenings, she sits out on the porch, reading until the sun sinks in the sky and the light begins to fade. She reminds me of the owls in the woods that fly away whenever they see anyone. When we head down Main Street, she hurries with a walk that is more of a run, waving if one of her old high school friends calls hello but never stopping to chat.

She avoids the Starline Diner. Too sociable. Too many people she might know from the past. The last time we went in together it was my birthday and I begged for a special treat. Maybe because I've always had piles of cakes and pies and cupcakes, the dessert I yearn for is ice cream. It is perhaps my favorite food in the world, what I imagine real pixies would eat, if they ate anything at all. I love the shivery feeling eating ice cream gives you, as if you were surrounded by a cold cloud.

My mother and I sat in a corner booth and ordered ice cream sodas to celebrate my turning twelve. Twelve is a mysterious number and I'd always thought something exceptional would happen to me after that birthday, so I was feeling cheerful about the future, which is not usually my nature. I ordered chocolate, and my mother asked for strawberry. The waitress was a friendly woman named Sally Ann who'd known my mother growing up. She came over to our table, and when I blurted out that it was my birthday she told me that she and my mother had been best friends when they were twelve. She gazed sadly at my mother. "And now all these years have passed right by and I never hear a word from you, Sophie." Sally Ann seemed genuinely hurt that the friendship had ended. "Why are you hiding up there on Old Mountain Road when all your friends miss you?"

"You know me," my mother said. "I always kept to myself."

"That is not one bit true," Sally Ann insisted. She turned to me. "Don't believe her. Your mother was the most popular girl in Sidwell, but then she went off to New York City and when she came back she wasn't the same. Now she doesn't talk to anyone. Not even me!"

As soon as Sally Ann was called back to the counter, my mother whispered, "Let's go." We sneaked out the door before our ice cream sodas appeared. I don't know if my mother had tears in her eyes, but she looked sad as could be. Even sadder when Sally Ann ran after us and handed us our sodas to go in paper cups.

"I didn't mean to chase you away," Sally Ann apologized. "I was just saying I missed you. Remember when we were in ballet class together and we always went to the dance studio early so we could have the whole place to ourselves and dance ourselves silly?"

My mother smiled at the memory. I could see who she once was in the expression that crossed her face.

"I always liked Sally Ann," she said as we drove away. "But I could never be honest with her now, and how can you have a friend if you can't tell her the truth?"

I understood why my mother couldn't have friends, and why my fate was the same. I couldn't tell the truth either, though sometimes I wanted to shout it out so much my mouth burned. I could feel the words I longed to say stinging me, as if I'd swallowed bees that were desperate to be free. *This is who I am.* That's what I'd shout. *I may not have a life like you do, but I'm Twig Fowler, and I have things to say!*

On most evenings and weekends we stayed at home and didn't venture out. That was our life and our fate and it wouldn't do any good to complain. I suppose you could call it the Fowler destiny. But I knew Sally Ann was right. It hadn't always been this way. I'd seen the photographs and the scrapbooks in a closet up in the attic. My mother used to be different. In high school she was on the track team and in the theater club. She always seemed to be surrounded by friends, ice-skating or having hot chocolate at the Starline Diner. She raised money for Sidwell Hospital's children's center by organizing a Bake-a-thon, baking one hundred pies in a single week that were sold to the highest bidders.

When she finished high school she decided she wanted to see the world. She was brave back then, and independent. She kissed her parents good-bye and left town on a Greyhound bus. She was young and headstrong and she'd dreamed of being a chef. Not someone who cooked in the Starline Diner, which she did on weekends all through high school. A real chef in a world-class restaurant. Pastries were always her specialty. She ran off to London and then to Paris, where she lived in tiny apartments and took cooking classes with the best chefs. She walked along foggy riverbanks to farmers' markets where she bought pears that tasted like candy. At last she wound up in New York City. That was where she met my father. The most she would tell me was that a mutual acquaintance had thought they'd be perfect for each other, and as it turned out, they were. My father was waiting for her when her plane touched down, there to help her find her way in Manhattan. Before the taxi reached her new apartment, they'd fallen in love.

But they split up before my mother came back home for her parents' funeral—my grandmother and grandfather had been in a car crash in the mountains during mudslide season. It happened in the Montgomery Woods, where the trees are so old and tall it seems dark even at noontime and there are several hairpin turns that make your stomach lurch when you drive around them. It was terribly sad to lose my grandparents, even though I was just a little girl. I can remember them in bits and pieces: a hug, a song, laughter, someone reading me a fairy tale about a girl who gets lost and finds her way home through the forest by leaving bread crumbs or following the blue-black feathers of crows.

When we came to Sidwell I was in the backseat of the old station wagon, which barely made it to Massachusetts. I was only a small child, but I remember looking out the window and seeing Sidwell for the first time. My mother changed our names back to Fowler from whatever my father's name was and she took over the farm. Every year she hires people traveling through town who need work. They pick apples and make the cider, but she does all the baking herself. If she's ever invited to a party or a town event, she writes a note politely declining. Some people say we're snobs because we once lived in New York and we expect life to race by with thrills like it does in Manhattan, and others say we think we're too good for a little town where not much ever changes. Still others wonder what happened to the husband my mother found and lost in New York.

People in Sidwell can talk all they want. They don't know the whole story. And if we're smart, they never will.

When we came home from New York I wasn't the only one in the backseat of the car.

That's why we arrived after dark.

Though I'm shy, I know most people in Sidwell, at least by name, except for the new neighbors who were just moving into the house at the edge of our property. I'd heard about them, of course, at the General Store. I'd biked over to the store to deliver two boxes of strawberry cupcakes that were so sweet I had what seemed like an entire hive of bees trailing after me. There's a group of men who have their coffee at the General Store before they head out to work. I secretly think of them as the Gossip Group. They're carpenters and plumbers, and even the postman and the sheriff sometimes join in. They have opinions on everything and comments about everyone and they tell jokes about the monster they seem to think are funny: *What do you do with a green monster? Wait for it to ripen. How does a monster play football? He crosses the ghoul line.*

When the talk turns serious, some of the men vow that one of these days there's going to be a monster hunt and that will be the end of things disappearing in town. That sort of conversation always gives me the chills. Thankfully, most of the recent talk has been about whether the woods will be turned into a housing development—over a hundred acres owned by Hugh

Montgomery. People see even less of him than they do of us. The Montgomerys live in Boston and only come to Sidwell on holidays and weekends. They used to spend summers here, but now people say they're more likely to go to Nantucket or France. Lately, there have been trucks up in the forest, early in the morning, when the hollows are misty. Soon enough folks figured out that the water and soil were being tested. That's when people in town became suspicious about Montgomery's intentions.

I had other things to think about, so I didn't pay too much attention. The woods had always been there and I figured they always would be. I was more focused on the fact that new neighbors were moving into the property next to our orchard. That was big news to us. We'd never had neighbors before. Mourning Dove Cottage, deserted for ages, always had doves nesting nearby. You could hear them cooing when you walked up to the overgrown yard that was filled with brambles and thistles. The cottage had broken windows and a caving-in roof that was covered with moss. It was a grim and desolate place, and most folks avoided the area. It's not just the Gossip Group fellows who say a witch lived there long ago. Everyone agrees that the Witch of Sidwell was a resident until she had her heart broken. When she disappeared from our village, she left a curse behind.

Kids may stand at the edge of the lawn and listen to the doves, they may dare one another to go up to the porch, but they run away when one of those rare black Sidwell owls flies across the distance, and they never go inside. I made it onto the porch one time. I opened the front door, but I didn't step over the threshold, and afterward I had nightmares for weeks.

Every August a play about the Witch of Sidwell is performed at Town Hall by the youngest group in the summer camp. When I was little, the drama teacher, Helen Meyers, wanted me to be the witch.

"I have a feeling you'll be the best Agnes Early we've ever had," she told me. "You have natural talent, and that doesn't come along often."

It was an honor to be given the starring role and I was proud to have been chosen. From the time I was tiny I longed to be an actress, and maybe even write plays when I got older. But my mother came down to rehearsals before I'd said my last line—*Do not pry into my business if you know what's best for you and yours!*

Upset, she took Mrs. Meyers aside. "My daughter is the witch?"

"She's a natural," Mrs. Meyers cheerfully announced.

"A natural witch?" My mother seemed confused and insulted.

"Not at all, my dear. A natural actress. Not many have true talent, but when they do, it's usually the shy ones. They just bloom onstage."

"I'm afraid my daughter won't be able to continue on," my mother told Mrs. Meyers.

I was so shocked I couldn't say a word. All I could do was watch, speechless, as my mother informed the drama teacher that I would not be in the play, not even as a member of the chorus. I had a friend back then, my first and only one, a boy I shared my lunch with every day. We were both shy, I suppose, and we were both fast runners. What I remember is that he came to stand beside me on the day I left camp, and he held my hand, because I had already started to cry. I was only five, but I was so disappointed that when we got home, I sobbed until my eyes were rimmed red. My mother sat beside me and tried her best to console me but I turned away from her. I didn't understand how she could be so mean. At that moment I thought of myself as a rose cut down before I could bloom.

That night my mother brought dinner to my room,

homemade tomato soup and toast. There was a Pink peach berry pie, but I didn't touch my dessert. I could tell that my mother had been crying, too. She said there was an unfortunate reason I couldn't be in the play. We were not like other people in town. We knew well enough not to mock a witch. Then my mother whispered what a witch could do if you crossed her. She could enchant you, which is what she did to our family more than two hundred years ago. Because of this curse we were still paying the price. I could write my own plays and perform them up in the attic, making up stories, dressing in old clothes I'd found in a metal trunk. But I could not ridicule the Witch of Sidwell.

My mother had a look in her eye I'd come to know. When she made a decision, there was no going back. I could beg and plead, but once her mind was made up that was that.

We baked the Pink apple cupcakes to be served at the party after the play, but we did not attend the performance. Instead we sat on a park bench in the center of Sidwell as the dark fell across the sky. We could hear the bell above Town Hall as it chimed six. We could hear an echo as the audience applauded for the new witch once the play had begun.

I think that evening was the beginning of my feeling lonely, a feeling I carried folded up, a secret I could never tell. From then on, I didn't cry when I was disappointed. I just stored up my hurts, as if they were a tower made of fallen stars, invisible to most people, but brightly burning inside of me.

It was late spring when the new people moved into Mourning Dove Cottage, the time of year when the orchard was abloom with a pink haze. For months there had been carpenters hammering and sawing as they worked away on the cottage, fixing shingles onto the roof, removing broken glass, and restoring the tumbledown porch. Some of the Gossip Group had been employed by the new owners of Mourning Dove, and they loved to tell people at the General Store how much they were charging the newcomers for their renovations. They were city people, outsiders, and so they paid top dollar for their rebuilt roof and a non-sagging porch. I thought this wasn't very neighborly, and I could tell that Mr. Stern felt the same way.

"If you're honest with someone he'll be honest with you," he told the men who gathered near his checkout counter, but I think I was the only one paying attention.

In this season I always collect flowering branches, enough to fill every one of our vases so the scent of apple blossoms will filter through our house, from the kitchen all the way to the attic. I spend hours curled up in my favorite tree, an old, twisted one that is thought to be the original apple tree planted in Sidwell. It's knobby, with velvety black bark, but I think the branches are like arms. I read books and do my homework up here. I take naps under a bower of leaves. In my dreams men and women can fly and birds live in houses and sleep in beds. Sometimes the doves nest above me and I can hear the cooing of their fledglings as I doze peacefully.

I was up in my favorite tree the day I heard the moving van rumbling down the dirt road beyond our orchard, with a car following behind as our new neighbors headed toward their new home. Dust rose in little whirlwinds as the truck came closer, and from the car's open window there was the sound of girls singing.

I sat still and squinted. It must be like this to be a bird looking down at the strange things people do. The newcomers had rooms full of oak furniture and silky rugs that shimmered with color. There were two parents who looked friendly as they bustled in and out of the house, and a shaggy collie dog they called Beau. The older of the two sisters was named Agate. She appeared to be about sixteen, with blond hair that reached to her shoulders and a laugh I could hear all the way across the orchard. The other one, Julia, was my age. She raced about collecting boxes that had her name scrawled across them from where the movers had placed them on the grass. "Mine," she'd call out as she lugged each newly discovered box up to the porch. At one point, she kicked off her shoes and did a little dance in the grass. She looked like someone who knew how to have fun, a lesson I needed to learn. I couldn't help but think that if I were a different person, I would want her as a friend. But a friend might want to come to our house, and when I said that wasn't possible, she might want to know why, and then I'd have to lie and I'd feel the stinging in my mouth that I always had when I didn't tell the whole truth.

I couldn't tell anyone about my brother, so there was no point to it really.

No one even knew I had a brother, not my teachers or classmates, not even the mayor, who vowed he knew every single person in Sidwell and had shaken every hand. I'd seen the mayor not long ago at the General Store, where he was discussing the weather and the future of the Montgomery Woods. He hadn't come out for or against the plan to develop the woods and put in houses and stores and maybe even a mall, although there probably weren't enough people in Sidwell to shop there. Being wishy-washy seemed to keep the mayor in office. The last time I'd seen him in town, he'd shaken my hand and looked into my eyes in a piercing way, then insisted I tell him my name and age, even though I had met him half a dozen times before. "Twig. Twelve years old, and tall at that! I'll remember your face and your name and your age because that's what a mayor does!" But every time I saw him after that he'd narrow his eyes as if trying to think of who I might be. I didn't blame him. I considered myself to be a shadow, a footstep in the woods that disappeared, a twig no one noticed. It was better that way. My mother always said the only way for us to stay in Sidwell was to live in the corners of everyday life.

I was tucked so far into a corner I was just about invisible.

I probably would have never met the Hall sisters and we might have remained strangers forever, if I hadn't fallen out of the tree and broken my arm. I leaned forward on a branch that was split through. Ordinarily, I would have been more careful, but I was concentrating on my new neighbors, and the wavering branch broke the rest of the way with me on it. I went down hard and fast. I cried out before I could stop myself. The collie came running over, followed by the Hall sisters. There I was, sprawled out on the ground, so embarrassed I could only stutter a hello.

My full name is Teresa Jane Fowler but everyone calls me Twig because of how much time I spend climbing apple trees, although now it seemed climbing was over for me, at least for a while.

"Don't move! Our father is a doctor," the older sister, Agate, announced. She raced back to the cottage, leaving me there with the collie and the girl my own age.

Julia introduced herself, and when I told her I was Twig from next door she nodded thoughtfully and said, "I wished there would be someone living right near us who was my age and it happened!"

She was dark, like me, only not as tall. I felt even worse about cutting my hair so short. Hers was long and straight, almost to her waist. We looked like opposite versions of each other.

"Does your arm hurt?" she asked.

"I'm fine." I wasn't one to let my feelings show. "Perfect, as a matter of fact."

Julia's face furrowed with concern. "I once broke my toe. I screamed so much I lost my voice."

"I'm really okay. I think I'll just walk home now." I was trying to be nonchalant, but my arm was throbbing. When I tried to move I gasped. The pain shot through me.

"Are you sure you're all right?"

"I am so not all right," I admitted.

"Scream. You'll feel better. I'll do it with you."

We let loose and screamed and all the doves floated up into the sky. They looked so beautiful up above us, like clouds.

Julia was right. I did feel better.

Dr. Hall ran out and examined me right there in the grass. He was tall and wore glasses. It was obvious that he'd had lots of practice making people feel better even when they were in pain.

I liked him right away; he seemed very knowledgeable but not overly worried, the way my mother was whenever something went wrong. She panicked at the idea of asking for help, but Dr. Hall made it seem like helping another person was the most natural thing in the world.

"We're going to take care of this before you can blink," he assured me. He had bright blue eyes and his hair was a little gray. "Can you move your fingers like a spider on a tabletop?" he asked. When I could he said, "Perfect!"

"You did say you were perfect." Julia grinned at me.

"Well, not in every way. Just in climbing trees. Or at least, I was."

"What about lifting your arm?" Dr. Hall asked. "How perfect is that?" I tried to raise it and winced. It was like an electric shock going through me.

Dr. Hall told me I probably had a small fracture. My arm would have to be x-rayed, then most likely set in a cast. The folks at the hospital would need my mother's permission. I told him our phone number, but when he tried to call no one answered. My mother was probably in the summer kitchen, a separate building beside the house where we had two huge ovens. The cider press was out there, and we usually stored baskets of apples that lasted through the winter. My mother didn't take her phone along in order to give her baking her full attention. Dr. Hall left a message for her to call the hospital as soon as she could, and then meet us in the emergency room. "No worries," he assured her in his message. "Nothing that can't be fixed."

"Let's go," he called out to everyone. "Time waits for no broken bones. Hospital run."

The whole family piled into the car, including the very comforting Mrs. Hall, who said, "Call me Caroline. No stuffy stuff for me." She had dark hair, cut short like mine, but she didn't look like a pixie, she just looked fashionable, as if someone in a movie had wandered into Sidwell.

They drove me to the hospital, with the dog, Beau, along for the ride. I looked out the window, afraid to talk too much. They chattered away, a real family, and I may have been a little jealous. I always wished my family could have done even the simplest things together. Just going for a car ride all together seemed extraordinary to me.

When we passed the General Store I noticed something you don't see every day in Sidwell: graffiti sprayed onto the brick wall. I had to blink to make certain I was seeing straight. There was a painted mouth with fangy teeth, all jagged and fierce. The jarring oversized words underneath read: *DON'T TAKE OUR HOME AWAY.*

It was such a sad and angry image a shiver ran through me. Some members of the Gossip Group were out there examining the paint and they didn't look too pleased. I thought Mr. Stern would just about faint when he saw his store defaced, and I wondered who in Sidwell

would have the nerve to paint that message. I was re-
lieved that the Halls didn't notice when we passed by.

At the hospital, everyone seemed to know Dr. Hall.
We were rushed into the emergency room because my
mother had already phoned to give her permission for
me to be treated. She was on her way. I was certain she
was worried beyond belief. Julia sat with me while the
orthopedist examined me. I had X-rays, then the doctor applied the cast to my arm. When she was finished,
we waited for the cast to dry, tapping on it to mark its
progress.

Julia was the first to sign my cast, with a purple
marker she had in her backpack. *To my friend the tree
climber, from Julia Hall.* Then Agate came to sign it as
well. She smelled of jasmine cologne. Julia whispered it
was the scent her sister always wore. Agate pushed back
her long pale hair and wrote *Agate Early Hall, your neigh-
bor* in tiny, beautiful script.

All three of us were drinking hot chocolates that
we'd bought in the vending machine when my mother
came to fetch me. She'd left home as soon as she got the
message and arrived wearing a raincoat over her old bak-

ing clothes, which were splattered with flour and cinnamon. She had pulled on the high rubber boots she used on rainy days. Since it wasn't yet apple season, she'd been in the middle of baking strawberry rhubarb pies. Her hands were pink and flour was dusted across her face in powdery white streaks. Despite the worry all over her face, she was still the most beautiful mother in town.

She couldn't thank Dr. and Mrs. Hall enough, insisting she would bring them a pie to express her gratitude. She hugged me tight and I hugged her back with my good arm and assured her I was fine. Or at least, I would be soon.

"She's perfect," Julia said. I grinned at her because being perfect was now a joke just between the two of us.

My mother wanted to see for herself. She came closer so she could examine my cast. I thought she would tell me how disappointed she was in me for bringing our neighbors into our situation, but instead she frowned when she saw the names written out. Julia said hello and introduced herself and started talking about how much she liked Sidwell, but my mother didn't seem to hear a word. She was staring at the beautiful Agate.

"Agnes Early," she said in a cold voice.

I'd never heard her sound like that. There were

blotches of red on my mother's cheeks. Her eyes were narrowed with suspicion.

"It's Agate." Agate left out the part about her middle name being Early, most likely because of the dark look on my mother's face.

My mother collected my belongings and tugged me toward the door. "We have to be going," she said in a no-nonsense tone. "Right now."

"Thank you!" I called to Agate and Julia, who both seemed confused over our hurried departure. We went right past Dr. and Mrs. Hall in the corridor as if we didn't even know them, when they'd pretty much saved me. "We hope to see you soon!" Mrs. Hall called. "Maybe for dinner!"

My mother waved, but didn't answer, not to say *Great, we'd love to,* nor to tell the truth, *No, we never accept invitations.* We went into the elevator and stood in silence as the doors closed behind us.

In the parking lot, Beau woofed at me from the back of the Halls' car and he wagged his tail, but we had already clambered into my mother's car and we quickly pulled away, back onto the road.

That night I was told never to go to Mourning Dove Cottage again. My arm had been broken, my mother said meaningfully. Who knew what might happen next?

"That house brings bad luck to our family," she announced. "And likely those people do, too."

"But they're really nice. And Julia's already invited me. If I don't go, she'll think I'm a snob."

"I wish it was different, Twig, but our families can never have anything to do with one another." My mother gazed at my arm. "I do not expect you to see those girls again. They're related to Agnes Early."

She was the Witch of Sidwell, who had lived at Mourning Dove, the relative Agate was named after.

The one who'd set a curse on our family over two hundred years ago.

CHAPTER TWO

The Distance Between Us

My brother James's room was in the attic. He was nearly seventeen, four years older than I am. He should have been a junior in high school, but my mother had homeschooled him all his life. He was smarter than anyone I knew. He'd taught himself French and Spanish and Latin and was already at a college level in most of his courses. He'd read every book in my grandfather's library. He knew I loved plays, and sometimes for my entertainment he would recite speeches from *Hamlet* at top speed, faster and faster, until we both fell down laughing. When my mother could no longer teach him mathematics or science because he'd far surpassed her knowledge in these fields, she bought him his own computer so he could take online courses at the university.

James was brilliant and funny and he had no idea how good-looking he was. I don't think he'd ever looked in a mirror. He never believed me when I said if he went to Sidwell High he'd have girls following him down the halls. "Sure, Twig," he'd say to me, and if I tried to argue with him he'd just shake his head and say, "No way." So I just gave up trying to convince him that in our family, he'd gotten all the looks. He had long dark hair and hazel eyes that changed color depending on his mood—green when he was happy, gray and moody most of the time, black when things went seriously wrong. He was tall and loyal and he had a smile that snuck up on you and made you forgive him almost anything.

James should have been on the football team, he was that strong, or been the star of the school play, he was that good-looking, or become a tennis champion, he was that quick and coordinated. It was so unfair that he couldn't do any of these things that I got furious just thinking about it. I ranted and raved and said we should run away, into the woods the way people did in fairy tales, finding their way through the forest in search of treasure. James listened to me, then he told me the world was not a fair place and we couldn't just run away from our lives. If everyone got what he or she deserved there would be no hunger, and no sadness, and there would certainly be no one like him, a boy who'd been locked away for his own good.

The men of the Fowler family have carried the same curse ever since Agnes Early put a spell on the one she was meant to marry. That man was my four-times-great-grandfather Lowell.

What he did to hurt her so, I didn't know, but I knew the effects on our family. This is the secret we kept, which divided us from all others. Agnes Early set her spell to work, and ever since, the men in our family have had wings.

You might imagine it would be a gift to be able to fly. In some ways it was.

James had flown between snowflakes, he told me, he'd covered distances no man could walk in a single day. He'd sat on clouds and been cloaked in mists. Early on he had learned the language of birds, and when he called to them they would answer.

"They're saying it will rain tonight," James informed me when some blue jays flew by. "They know when to leave New England," he would say of the geese calling as they passed overhead. "They're headed to Florida. They'll follow the coastline and stop in North Carolina." My brother's eyes would light up. "Imagine flying all that way? That's freedom."

It was a miracle to live as birds do, except for one thing: Anyone seen in flight would surely be captured, perhaps even shot down like a crow flying above a cornfield. It's always dangerous to be different, to appear as a monster in most people's eyes, even from a distance. That was why our mother didn't want James to be found out and why she had forbidden him to fly.

No one in our town knew my brother existed. As far as they were concerned, Sophie Fowler had come back from New York City with one child, and that child was me. My mother always said all our secrecy was to protect James, but sometimes I wondered if protecting someone might also ruin his life.

Because he could never go out, he had built a gym for himself so he could stay in shape. I'd bought most of the materials at the General Store, a little at a time, with money saved from both our allowances. It wasn't as if we had much to spend it on anyway.

"Hey, Twig," one of the Gossip Group had called the last time I went to pick up some tools and rope. "What are you building? A tiger trap?"

The men thought this was very funny. I paid for the rope and a hammer and nails and said nothing, but inside I was simmering. When they kept on teasing me, wondering if it was a bear I was after, or maybe an elephant, I blurted out, "I thought I'd catch the Sidwell Monster."

The men grew quiet, but from the looks on their faces I knew I had better be careful. The monster was no joke to them. I knew some of them thought there should be an official monster hunt now that the creature had grown bold enough to take the shirts right off people's clotheslines and drink bottles of milk that had been delivered to the back entrance of the elementary school. I'd heard that some Sidwell citizens thought the monster was behind the graffiti on Mr. Stern's store. I knew that wasn't true. But the Gossip Group clearly thought otherwise.

"Not a bad idea, Twig," a man named Jack Bellows said. He was one of the carpenters working over at Mourning Dove Cottage. "Now that he's stealing things, who knows what the monster will do next? Maybe he'll start walking inside our front doors to take whatever suits him. Maybe we'll open our eyes and there he'll be, standing over our beds. What will we do then?"

The men started to grumble about plans to hunt the monster this summer. I didn't like what I was hearing. It sounded like a lot of fear and prejudice to me.

"Actually I'm making a mega–jump rope," I said. "I don't believe in monsters."

That calmed things down. If a twelve-year-old girl wasn't frightened then a group of grown men looked pretty silly to be so rattled by something no one had ever seen or heard.

"Don't jump so high you hit the moon," Mr. Stern said as I was leaving.

I smiled then. "I won't."

I liked Mr. Stern. He always said the reason my mother's pies and cakes were his store's best sellers was because she was the best baker in New England, maybe even the best in the country.

It took two months for my brother to build his gym, and when he was done it was worthy of a circus ac-robat. He practiced for hours on the rings and the trapeze, walking on a wire so thin it seemed he was walking on air.

"Hey, you," he'd say when I came up the stairs.

"Hey, you," I'd say back with a grin.

We were always on each other's side, loyal at all times. I never said a word to my mother even though I knew that James sneaked out at night. It was after dark when the woods were most filled with magic, when there were fireflies and the mist was rising from the streams. Another secret of ours, one I'd never tell: He sometimes brought me with him. I think our mother would have flipped if she found out that I knew what it felt like to dart through raindrops, to follow herons over the flat water of the lake, to rise above the town of Sidwell when every window was dark and the bell at Town Hall chimed so far below us it sounded like a child's toy.

It had begun when I was five years old, right after my mother took me out of the play. I had always begged and pleaded with my brother, and when he saw how disappointed I was not to be the Witch of Sidwell, he finally gave in. I think he'd always wanted to share how beautiful and blue the earth appeared from above.

That first time, I clung to him and closed my eyes. I had to stop myself from crying out when he leapt into the starry night sky, but when I opened my eyes I knew the secret my brother carried with him, the amazement of flying through clouds, skimming over the trees, making our way through the labyrinth of the forest, counting stars as the night glimmered around us.

Sometimes whole flocks of birds followed in our wake. The dozens of abandoned baby birds James had raised recognized him, as if he was their brother as well as mine, an odd large bird with a human face who knew how to speak their language. James was currently caring for a baby owl that had injured its wing in a fall from its nest. The owl sat on his shoulder and ate bits of cereal from his fingers. James had named him Flash because his big yellow eyes seemed like a flashlight beam. Flash's wing was still healing, so mostly he hopped around. He had a way of tilting his head that made it appear he understood every word you said to him.

On one of our flights, James had shown me where the Sidwell owls could be found in the Montgomery Woods. I always go back there when I go on hikes. I hoot and call, and occasionally I'll spy an owl peering down from a tree. Our owls are called saw-whet owls. They're as small as robins, and they usually hide in the foliage when they spy people nearby, but my brother was different and the owls knew it. They trusted him and maybe because of that, they had begun to trust me.

"They're unique," my brother had explained. "I've

never seen owls like these in any reference books." They were all black as crows. "Other saw-whets are brown. It must be a genetic mutation."

Some things could only be found in Sidwell, it seemed: Pink apples, black owls, and my brother, James.

When I got home from the hospital, I held up my arm so James could see my cast. He was balanced on one of the large aerial rings he'd recently installed. He so excelled on the trapeze that the General Store didn't have everything he needed, and I had ordered new equipment from circus-supply stores.

James's expression shifted when he saw I'd been injured. He dropped to the floor. "Did someone hurt you?" He was always fiercely protective. I'd told him about the way kids sometimes made fun of me, using my nickname against me. *Skinny as a twig, tall as a twig, dumb as a twig.* Nothing terribly original; still, it hurt. But that was a long time ago, back when I was in elementary school. Now everyone just ignored me. I wasn't worth the time to be teased.

"It's not serious. And I did it to myself. I fell out of a tree."

"I should have been there. I could have caught you."

"Well, lucky for me, the Hall sisters were there."

James was instantly curious. "The new neighbors?"

I nodded. "They sort of rescued me. Julia's the one who's my age. Agate is older. Almost your age. She has blond hair and she smells like jasmine and she only wears black."

I realized I'd said too much. I stopped blabbing about the Hall girls. I'd made James remember how lonely he was. He kept asking questions, wanting to hear more about them, especially Agate. What grade was she in, where did she come from, what did I say was the scent of the perfume she wore? He had a far-off look, so I didn't tell him everything. I knew it would only make him feel worse. I skipped over how beautiful Agate was and stuck with stories about what a mess their yard was and how smart Beau was, because I knew James had wanted a dog forever. Still, he always came back to asking about Agate. Maybe he had a dream girl and maybe he thought she was that dream come true.

"I wish," James began. Then he stopped. He didn't have to say it aloud. I knew he wished he was like everyone else. A boy who could visit the girl next door and see for himself what she looked like. "Wishes are worthless," my brother muttered as he turned away.

I heard a bitterness that hadn't been there before.

Something was changing inside him. He'd had enough of following the rules. I could read it in his eyes, gray as a storm.

James had a theory about caged birds, one he hoped to prove when he became a scientist someday. He believed that all birds that had their freedom taken from them eventually lost their voices. Once that happened, they could never again find their true song.

In the past months, I'd wondered if that was happening to James. A sort of hopelessness had sifted down and had come between us. When I asked him to take me into the woods, he said he was too tired, yet I often heard him go out at night. It was clear he didn't want my company anymore. We had always played board games after supper; now he said he'd rather be alone. He was withdrawing. I think it was getting harder for him to accept his fate.

Like a bird in a cage, he grew silent.

As my mother and I went about our lives we sometimes forgot he was there. When he was younger James would ask my mother when he could go to school like everyone else, when he could go into town, and of course the question that was on my mind as well: When would we see our father? James had stopped asking long ago, and now I was afraid he had given up.

Every once in a while I went up to the attic to ask him to do a speeded-up Shakespearean speech. I begged and begged until he gave in. *To be, or not to be,* he began. *Whether 'tis nobler in the mind to suffer the slings and arrows of outrageous fortune, or to take arms against a sea of troubles.* He spoke so fast the words slurred together, and before long we were both laughing. It was a relief to hear James laugh again, and even more of a relief to know after all this time of being caged, he still hadn't lost his voice.

I liked to walk to school because it gave me time to think. You might imagine I'd spent enough time by myself, but somehow in the woods it was different. I felt at home surrounded by the creatures that lived here. There were chipmunks and quail and scores of field mice. No outsiders, no monsters, only beauty all around me. I could climb onto a crag and look down at Sidwell. It was the perfect New England town, with a magic all its own. Sometimes it seemed that we were cut off from the rest of the world and time itself moved differently here. If enchantment could be found anywhere, it would surely be in the Berkshires, where the woods were so green and deep, and a mist rose from the streams that crisscrossed the meadows so that even those of us without wings felt as if we were walking through the clouds.

I went through the woods until I could cut through to the end of Old Mountain Road. Then I walked along the asphalt with the sun beating down on my shoulders. Whenever I heard a car coming up behind me, I'd jump into the tall grass and wait for the driver to pass. I did so carefully, because once I'd almost stepped on three baby field mice waiting for their mother to return with their breakfast.

On the Monday after I broke my arm there was a friendly beeping of a horn as I walked along. When I turned there was the Halls' car. Mrs. Hall—I still couldn't call her Caroline—and the girls waved. They looked much too fashionable for Sidwell, but all the same they were so warm and cheerful, as if their rescue after my fall had made us friends forever. As soon as I thought the word *friends* I grew dizzy. My heart thudded. I think I looked the way a deer by the side of the road does when it's startled by the sudden appearance of human life.

Julia rolled down her window. "Your chariot has arrived. Hop in."

I hesitated. I wanted to ride to school with the Hall girls. Maybe then I wouldn't be such an outcast. Maybe I'd even call myself Teresa instead of Twig. But I knew my mother wouldn't approve. No invitations were to be accepted, not of any sort. And most assuredly there was to be no contact with the witch's family, not under any circumstances, not after what had happened to us two hundred years ago.

"I think I need the exercise." As if walking two miles to school were an Olympic feat. "Thanks anyway."

I walked on, more slowly than usual. My one chance of having a friend and I'd blown it. The car kept pace with me.

"How's your broken arm?" Julia called.

"Still broken!"

"Well, you look marvelous!" Agate chimed in.

"Super-duper," Mrs. Hall agreed from behind the steering wheel.

"Perfect." Julia grinned.

Our joke cheered me up. I'd been embarrassed to go to school with my cast, thinking I looked like even more of a gawk than usual, but the Halls made me forget about that. The cast wasn't really so bad. The car stopped and the doors swung open. Agate and Julia hugged their mother good-bye, then came running to join me.

"We need the exercise, too," Agate said. "We're too lazy."

"We're here to change our lives," Julia added. "So we might as well start by walking."

We trotted along, arm in arm. At first I was afraid that my mother might drive past on her way to the grocery and spy me with the girls, but after a while I just stopped worrying. I wasn't inside Mourning Dove Cottage, but on a public road, which was there for anyone to walk upon, even the Hall sisters, even me.

"We were so hoping to see you and we did!" Julia said. "Things just kind of happen here in Sidwell, don't they? Like magic."

"Like it's meant to be," I agreed.

"Like it's perfect," Julia and I said at the very same time.

"You two are peas in a pod." Agate grinned. "What is so funny about the word *perfect*?"

"Nothing." Julia aimed a smile at me. She had on a red T-shirt with I AM WHO I AM printed in black letters, some faded jeans, and old-school black-and-white sneakers. I had on my favorite jeans and a white T-shirt my brother had ordered for my birthday. *Owls Rule* was in swirly type, and a silk-screened black owl decorated the front and back. We were practically dressed like twins except that her T-shirt was black and red and mine was black and white. Agate, on the other hand, was surprisingly elegant, especially for a town like Sidwell. Her pale hair was drawn back with a velvet headband and she wore a black dress and ballet slippers. She certainly didn't look like anyone else in our school. When Julia saw me gazing at her sister's clothes, she told me Agate designed and sewed everything she wore.

"Someday she'll be famous," Julia confided. "And I'll model all of her clothes. When I'm not busy being an artist."

"Where did you live before this?" I asked the sisters, thinking the answer might be Paris or Rome.

"Brooklyn," Agate said.

That explained how stylish she and Mrs. Hall were. They were New Yorkers, something I'd always sort of considered myself to be. I'd been born there, after all.

"Our father got a job at Sidwell Hospital. That's why we're here. He's the chief of surgery," Agate said proudly.

"That's not why we're here," Julia added. "It's because of me."

"No it isn't." Agate gave her sister a little shove, but her expression was concerned.

"It's true and you know it. I hated our old school. No one liked me."

"Who could not like you?" I said.

Julia threw me a grateful look. "I'm bad at sports," she admitted. "In my old school, that gave some people a good reason to treat me like an outcast. If there was ever a team, I was picked last, not that I blamed them. But they didn't have to be so mean about it."

"Mean people are meaningless," Agate said. "I've told you that a hundred times."

I was accustomed to people acting as if I didn't exist, but I couldn't believe anyone would purposely be cruel to Julia. She was so easy to like.

"That won't happen here," I said. Sidwell was a pretty friendly place. Too friendly, my mother always warned, for people like us.

As we walked to school I began to think that if Julia wanted a new start, she had better stay away from me. Everyone in Sidwell knew I wasn't coming to their houses and they weren't coming to mine. They were well aware I didn't attend parties or dances or go to the Main Street Cinema with everyone else on Saturday afternoons, though I really was dying to see some of the movies I heard people talking about. By now my classmates had realized I was the person most likely to be ignored. I wasn't just unpopular, I was nothing more than a glimmer of a girl people saw but never really noticed. "Oh, hi, Twig," someone might say in a surprised sort of way if they came upon me, as if they had stumbled over the root of a tree or an old potted plant. Julia would definitely have better luck if she wasn't seen with me. The truth was, I didn't want her to find out what a nothing I was.

When we got to school, I announced I had a meeting with a teacher and took off running. I didn't want to jinx Julia and Agate by their association with me. I called back, "Good luck!" and acted as if I didn't hear Julia calling, "Wait up!"

I just kept going.

I caught sight of the Hall sisters several times during the day, always surrounded by a crush of people. I wasn't surprised. Sidwell was such a small town that anyone new was immediately interesting, especially when they were as special as Agate or as funny and friendly as Julia. They had what they wanted on their very first day at school: a new life filled with friends. Exactly what I'd always wanted.

As usual, no one paid any attention to me. The only one who asked what had happened to my arm was my English teacher, Mrs. Farrell, who was such a huge fan of *Wuthering Heights* she had a cat named Emily Brontë. Mrs. Farrell had always been nice to me, and I think she felt a little sorry for me because I was always alone. She signed my cast, *Get well soon to a great student! From Mrs. Farrell and Emily Brontë.*

Thankfully it was my left arm that was banged up, so I managed with my schoolwork. I was happy for Agate and Julia that they were so instantly popular. I wouldn't have wanted to ruin that. I stayed out of their way. It's easy to keep to yourself if you hang back and always sit in the last row and slip around corners as if you were a ghost.

Instead of walking home on the road, where the Hall girls might catch up with me, I went through the Montgomery Woods. People said there were still bears in Sidwell, but I'd never run across one. I had spied raccoons and skunks and foxes, and I'd run across moles, which were shyer than I was, and boisterous turkeys. I must have looked like a twig to them, too, because they all ignored me.

Even though the Montgomerys had bought a huge section of the woods, aside from the old estate where they vacationed sometimes, it was still wilderness all around, no different than it had been hundreds of years earlier. Streams of lemony-yellow sunlight drifted in between the branches. There were ferns and swamp cabbage growing in the boggy places, stretches of watery land that were so darkly green they looked black. I found some bushes with thin fairy branches filled with wild raspberries that had ripened early. I picked some to bring home to James, and kept them in my pockets on the way back. I made a loop-de-loop around the owl nesting grounds.

That was when I saw more graffiti. It was on a huge boulder that had probably been in the same place since the Ice Age. There was the same blue spray paint I'd noticed in town on the wall of the General Store, the same fangy teeth of a monster, and the same writing: *DON'T TAKE OUR HOME AWAY.*

I ran the rest of the way, as fast as I could, which in my case is pretty fast. Raspberries fell from my pockets, but I didn't care. I went through ferns and past the trout orchids and the wild pink roses that grow everywhere in Sidwell. Even though I knew there was no such thing as a monster, someone was definitely in the woods, someone who didn't want to be seen and wanted people to stay out. I raced out of there so quickly I could have made the track team at school if I joined things. I had the same shivery feeling I'd had when I saw the blue graffiti in town. Almost as if someone were scribbling a message to me.

I didn't wait around to see if someone wanted to tell me something. And I didn't stop until I could see the road.

My mother made a pie to thank the Halls for taking such good care of me when I broke my arm. She'd promised she would, and she was always true to her word.

"But how do I send it over there?" She frowned, but even then she was beautiful. "If I go, they might invite me in for coffee, or ask how many children I have. I don't want to lie and I can't tell the truth." She sat down at the kitchen table, distraught, doing her best to puzzle out what to do next. It had been so long since she'd had anything to do with strangers that she'd forgotten how to act with people. She was flustered and nervous over one pie.

I tried to comfort her. "You could just say hello, thank you, and good-bye."

My mother laughed, but shook her head. "I'd be opening the door to being neighborly. You know I can't do that. One thing would lead to another, and before you knew it they'd be inviting us over for dinner and wondering why we never invited them here."

I couldn't help it, I was curious about the Halls. I wondered if Julia would still be as friendly now that so many people had clustered around her at school. Maybe she'd already found someone better to be her friend. My heart sank at the thought, even though I might have brought it upon myself when I disappeared at school.

My mother wasn't happy when I suggested that I could bring over the pie, but after I vowed I could run so fast I could slip the pie onto the porch, then take off at top speed, she agreed.

"Consider me a thief in reverse," I said.

My mother came to put her arm around me. "You are my darling, thoughtful girl," she said to me. "And you are definitely not a thief."

But someone in Sidwell was. While I walked through the orchard I thought of all the things that had gone missing in town. I'd heard one of the school librarians tell Mrs. Farrell that a flashlight had been taken from her car one Sunday morning, and a carpenter outside the General Store told his buddy that a box of nails had been pinched from the back of his truck on Memorial Day. If I left the pie on the Halls' porch, would it still be there when they came out?

I found myself at Mourning Dove Cottage in no time. The driveway was filled with workmen's trucks. It was pretty hectic and I was accustomed to getting in and out of places without being seen, so I tried to be as unassuming as possible. But as soon as I came through the trees Beau started barking like mad, then raced over to me. I laughed when the dog bumped against me, wanting me to pet him, even though I didn't have a free hand. I almost dropped the pie, but managed to balance it before it could fall.

"Good catch!" Mrs. Hall called.

She was out in the garden, if you could call it that. It was a large area filled with brambles and weeds, surrounded by a tumbledown wooden fence. Mrs. Hall wore a straw hat and heavy gloves. She waved, then held up a mixing bowl. It was yellow ceramic, the kind I'd seen in the Sidwell history room at Town Hall. "I just unearthed this. Isn't it lovely? Hardly a chip on it."

"It's the kind the colonists used," I told her. "Probably at least two hundred years old."

I'd spent a good deal of time at the history room. Miss Larch was the librarian there. She always joked she was a hundred years old and therefore knew more history than anyone in town. She had snow-white hair that was twisted up, and she usually wore a black dress with silver buttons and a long silver necklace with the keys to Town Hall hanging on the chain. Every time I went into the library, she would call out, "Why, if it isn't Teresa Jane!" as if just seeing me made her happy. Miss Larch used to teach history at the high school before she retired to volunteer at Town Hall. "I taught your mother when she was a girl. I must say, she was an excellent student. Always reading. She loved novels and cookbooks."

Miss Larch had invited me to tea several times. There was a hot plate set up on an old pine bureau, and she had some old blue-and-white china cups and silver spoons with mother-of-pearl handles. Miss Larch used a colonial teapot made of the same yellow ceramic Mrs. Hall found in her garden. There were also two dozen canisters of exotic teas I'd never heard of before: gunpowder, jasmine, yuzu, Marco Polo, cherry vanilla, black orchid. Teas that could chase away nightmares and those that could improve your memory and others that could make you laugh out loud with one sip. I always thanked Miss Larch but said I had to be on my way, even though I wished I could stay. That was who I was: Twig Fowler, who had to be going, who didn't have a minute to talk, who froze as soon as it seemed someone might ask a personal question, who could only mumble *Thank you*, then race out the door.

But I couldn't get away that easily when I was spotted in the Halls' yard. We were neighbors. The least I could do was be polite.

"You know an awful lot about Sidwell." Mrs. Hall came to greet me. "I'm impressed."

I shrugged. "I grew up here."

"So you did," Mrs. Hall said. Then she noticed the pie tin. "How lovely! There's nothing that can compare to real homemade pie."

I could see where Julia had inherited her outgoing nature. Julia had told me that her mother was a speech pathologist who worked with children who stuttered or had difficulty saying certain sounds. It was hard to be standoffish with her, especially when she hugged me and told me she hoped my arm wasn't hurting too badly. We were chatting so much I didn't even notice that I had followed her into Mourning Dove Cottage. I knew I was entering the territory of my family's enemy. I was on the verge of saying I had to go home, but when I walked through the door nothing terrible happened. I wasn't struck by lightning. I didn't fall flat on my face. I had to admit the truth to myself: I wanted to stay.

There were carpenters and plumbers and painters at work tearing up the old pipes and the rotten wood. I recognized Mr. Hendrix, the plumber, who had recently fixed our stopped-up kitchen sink. Several of the workmen from town called, "Hey there, Twig." I nodded a hello. I recognized some of them from the Gossip Group.

I could see that the interior of the house had been a wreck before the Halls had moved in. There were still cobwebs everywhere, and rings of water damage from winter storms had stained the ceilings and walls with odd splotches in the shapes of clouds and sheep. The floors, once coated with oxblood-red stain, had been refinished and were now a gleaming oak. The walls were gray and sooty with ash from ancient fires in the fireplace. They were lined with cracks, but cans of white paint were being opened. It would take quite a lot of work before the house looked livable again.

"This poor house," Mrs. Hall said as we stood in the front hallway. The cottage did seem sad, as if it had a broken heart along with stained ceilings and cracked plaster. "Our family has simply ignored it for generations. But we never sold it, and there must be a reason for that! I intend to bring it to life."

"It doesn't look very kept up," I blurted. "Sorry, Mrs. Hall. I don't mean to offend the house."

"Call me Caroline," Mrs. Hall reminded me. "And I don't know if a building can be offended. I'm certainly not. All the same, I think we're all going to love Mourning Dove Cottage. Why, I do already!"

She was so positive that I didn't want to mention that the last inhabitant had been a witch. I was about to leave before I overstayed my welcome, or before my mother realized I'd been gone for too long, or before Julia could decide she didn't want to be my friend. But before I could go, Julia came sprinting down the stairs, paint spattering her face.

"Just the person I wanted to see," she announced.

Since Julia had instantly been popular at school, I was surprised to hear this. Surely someone must have told her not to bother with Twig Fowler.

I looked a bit more closely at the paint on her face. Blue, the color of the graffiti. A wave of suspicion tugged at me.

"How's your arm?" Julia asked.

I only had three signatures on my cast. I couldn't

count the cat, Emily Brontë. Most people would have had every one of their friends sign and I was embarrassed not to have more names.

"People at school don't really notice me," I said. Meaning I wasn't in the in-crowd and didn't go to parties. I walked alone through the halls because I was a no one, so Julia and I might as well stop talking right now.

"People often don't notice something they've seen all their lives. That's what my mother says," Julia told me, wiping at the blue paint on her face with a damp paper towel.

"That's right." Mrs. Hall nodded. "They walk right past the roses growing by their front door and go to a florist's and pay good money for flowers that aren't half as pretty."

"I don't really care what people think anymore," Julia confided. "I make up my own mind." She grinned. "I'm from Brooklyn."

I decided to stay, just for a few minutes, long enough to have a slice of my mother's strawberry rhubarb pie. We went into the kitchen, and after a single bite, Mrs. Hall said it was the best she'd ever tasted.

"If your mother sold her pies in Brooklyn she'd be a millionaire." Julia took another big bite. "People would be lined up around the block and pay whatever she asked. Everyone would be pie-crazy and they'd applaud her whenever she walked down the street."

I couldn't deny my mother was the best baker around. "Wait till you taste our Pink apple pie this fall."

"It sounds heavenly." Mrs. Hall cut herself a second slice. "I wonder if your mother would ever share her recipe."

Just talking about my mother made me nervous to be in Mourning Dove Cottage. I'd broken my promise and had already been gone for nearly an hour. I was torn between wanting to stay and feeling I was being disloyal.

"She doesn't usually give out her recipes. They're kind of a family secret."

"Let's go upstairs," Julia suggested. "You have to see what I've done to my room."

I hesitated. It wasn't just the blue paint on Julia's face that concerned me. I imagined the witch stalking through these rooms, uttering curses, ruining the lives of everyone in our family.

"Race you!" Julia shouted. Like most runners, I took off once I heard a challenge. I forgot about my mother's warnings and the curse and the witch, and I reached the landing before Julia did.

"You are fast!" she said.

"It's not like I try. It's just my long legs."

Julia had been painting her room. The shade she'd chosen was a dark blue that reminded me of midnight. It was the opposite of the harsh electric-blue spray paint on the General Store and in the woods, as calm as the other blue was jarring. I felt a wave of relief.

"Let's make this room perfect," Julia suggested.

"Agreed." I was more than ready to help.

We dragged a ladder into the center of the room. Julia's plan was to stencil shimmery silver stars across the ceiling. She lent me a pair of sunglasses, then she put on some goggles, and we set to work, taking turns with a spray can of metallic paint. Again, I thought of the message I'd seen. *DON'T TAKE OUR HOME AWAY.*

"Did you buy this paint in Brooklyn?"

"Nope," Julia said. "In Sidwell. At Hoverman's Hardware Store."

The first star shone, as if it really had dropped through a hole in the roof to light up the room. Julia planned to paint on another star every day until she had entire constellations on her ceiling.

"Star light, star bright," Julia sang when we were done. "I hope this is the best summer ever."

I wished that, too, but I was afraid to say it aloud.

I had wished for a lot of things in the past: that James could have a life like other boys, that my father would come back, that I wouldn't hear my mother cry late at night. As my brother often said, for anyone in the Fowler family, wishes were worthless.

There was an old-fashioned seat built in beneath the window in Julia's room that overlooked our orchards. I'd always wanted to read while curled up in a window seat, and this one had blue pillows with a pattern of silver roses Agate had sewn. We made ourselves comfortable and compared the books we loved most. Our list included everything written by Edward Eager, of course, along with E. Nesbit and Ray Bradbury. I added *Wuthering Heights,* because of Mrs. Farrell. Even though I hadn't read it yet, it was on my list of must-reads. Julia suggested Emily Dickinson's poems, because she hadn't lived so far from Sidwell. Even though Emily Dickinson was something of a hermit, locking herself away in her room, sneaking out to collect wildflowers all by herself, she seemed like the kind of person you'd want to be friends with if you'd lived long ago, too.

Julia and I talked so much it took a while before I realized it was nearly dark. Shadows had begun to sift through the trees like pools of ink.

I stood up so fast the pillows fell onto the floor. I

picked them up, apologized for my clumsiness, then said, "I have to go." I felt like the White Rabbit in *Alice's Adventures in Wonderland,* in a wild panic, afraid of what might happen if I was late, which, frankly, I already was.

"Why can't you stay? You could have dinner and then I'll walk you halfway home."

"Absolutely not!" I sputtered without thinking. Julia looked stung and I could tell she was hurt. That was the last thing I wanted. "I'm sorry," I said. "I'd love to stay. But my mother wouldn't allow it. She didn't want me here in the first place."

"Why doesn't she like us? She doesn't even know us."

I explained as best I could. There had been a time when our families had been enemies and terrible things had been said and done. Hearts had been broken and fates led astray. I told her about the play at Town Hall and how once a year the youngest children at the summer camp told the story of Agnes Early, the Witch of Sidwell, and how they sang a song about how she put a curse on anyone who had harmed her, chanting three times that they wished the witch would disappear and never return.

"The play ends when the witch is pushed off a cliff made of papier-mâché," I told Julia. "Then everyone in town applauds."

"That's so rude!" Julia's face flushed with anger. "I've never heard of anything so mean!"

I tried to make excuses for Sidwell. "She was a witch, after all."

"It's still horrible to wish the worst on anyone. I'm sure she had her reasons. Maybe people hurt her feelings, the same way I was hurt in Brooklyn. A single word can feel like a rock being thrown at you."

I'd never thought of the witch's situation that way before, and when I said so Julia was pleased. Thinking of Agnes Early simply as someone who'd been hurt made me feel less frightened of her. And I didn't feel as nervous about the blue fangs I'd seen in town and in the woods. I was sure whoever was behind it had his reasons, just as the witch had.

"Let's meet on the road tomorrow to walk to school," I said. "Same time, same place."

"Perfect plan." Julia grinned.

I made my way downstairs, called out a good-bye to Mrs. Hall, and ran down the porch steps. I was feeling happy, like I was the most normal girl in Sidwell, or at least normal enough, and I didn't have a care in the world. But as soon as I got outside a wave of fear shot through me. Out on the lawn Agate Hall was staring at the orchard. She looked lit up, her face dreamy, her long arms wrapped around herself. It was chilly in the evenings and a mist threaded through the orchard. The moon was already rising. The stars appeared in a sky that was the exact color of Julia's bedroom.

I had the sense that something out of the ordinary had happened. All of the trees looked silver in the light, and there was a rushing sound, as if the wind had risen, but in fact the air was still.

Agate turned to me. Her eyes were wide, her cheeks flushed. She looked the way people do when they're just waking up from a dream.

"I saw him," she said, her tone soft. "The one they talk about. He's real."

We were both shivering, but for different reasons. I was afraid, but Agate seemed enchanted. I looked at her and I knew that for the first time in all these years, despite the danger, despite the curse, my brother had allowed himself to be seen.

CHAPTER THREE

Star-Crossed

You WOULD THINK AFTER TWO HUNDRED years a curse would have less of a hold and finally begin to wear off, like ink fading on an old piece of paper. But that wasn't the case.

In our family it had always been a tradition to remove the tiny wings on the day before a boy's first birthday. A mixture of herbs was added to the baby's milk, along with a dozen or more ingredients that were kept secret. Once the child drank this concoction, his wings would begin to disappear, shriveling little by little, inch by inch, until they fell off and feathers covered the floor.

But there was a price to pay to be like everyone else: From that time onward, the individual would be fragile, feverish and tired all the time, unable to play childhood games or even lift his arms over his head. The Fowler boys' bones would break easily, and some were confined to their beds. Even when they were grown men, their spines would ache every time there was a storm. My own grandfather had trouble walking and always used a cane. I remember coming to visit and sitting out on the porch with him, watching flocks of blackbirds fly past, as if there were inky clouds above us.

"That's freedom," he said to me, and even though I was little more than a baby, I heard the longing in his voice.

The herbal cure only worked before the child's first birthday. After that, the wings were set in place. The curse was unbreakable.

My mother was different from the rest of the Fowlers. Maybe because she had been out in the world and had witnessed how people lived their lives far from Sidwell, she refused the cure for my brother. She didn't care that every boy in our family for nearly two hundred years had had his wings removed. The process was dangerous and painful and she wouldn't stand for it.

She had her own methods when James was young. When we lived in New York City his wings were small enough that she could bind them before we went out; then she'd slip on an oversized sweatshirt. In crowded Manhattan no one noticed a pretty young mother, a little girl with dark hair in a stroller, and a handsome, serious five-year-old who didn't run off in the park as other boys did to play soccer or baseball, but instead stayed beside us, grounded, always well behaved, but set apart. He knew he was different even then.

I don't remember my father very much. He disappeared from our lives before I was old enough to know him, but my brother says that he often took us to the swings in Central Park. He would whisper to James that anyone lucky enough to experience flight was special. James would close his eyes and take a deep breath. Up in the air he finally felt free.

"What was he like?" I used to ask when James and I were alone.

"Tall, quiet, someone you could trust to catch you if you were up in the air."

But all I recalled was a shadow, and as the years passed, even the memory of that shadow seemed to be disappearing.

I was never quite sure what happened to my parents, or why they had separated. Every time I brought it up, my mother turned away.

One day I was thinking about my father while I was doing my homework in the history room at Town Hall. My class had been assigned to write about Sidwell's founding in 1683, and I was doing research about the town's first library. It had been situated in an old wooden cabin on the town green. The building still existed, but was currently used as a tourist center. People visiting Sidwell stopped here for maps and a list of sights they should see on their way to Lenox or Stockbridge. Recommended highlights were the Montgomery Woods, Last Lake, the Starline Diner, and the bell tower at Town Hall.

For some reason reading about the early days of Sidwell made me think about my family's early days in New York. I puzzled over how little I knew of my own family history, and how I longed for something I'd never even known and would probably never have. I started crying, something I'd never done in public before. I was especially embarrassed because Miss Larch was entertaining an elderly gentleman who wore a tweed jacket and carried a silver-tipped cane. He gazed over at me and made a clucking sound. I could tell he felt bad for me. The fact that someone I didn't even know pitied me made me feel worse.

Miss Larch whispered a few words to her companion and I heard him say, *Oh, yes, of course. Don't mind me.*

She brought over a freshly brewed cup of black orchid tea and sat across from me. The tea was especially fragrant. From that day on, it was my favorite. The scent reminded me of rainy days and libraries and a jumble of gardens where there were flowers in bloom.

"This particular blend is very good for sadness," Miss Larch said, urging me to try it.

"Won't your friend be upset to be left alone?" I asked, wiping at my eyes. I didn't really mind crying in front of Miss Larch. I probably knew her better than anyone else in Sidwell.

"Oh, Dr. Shelton is a very patient man," she assured me. "And very well educated. He won't mind entertaining himself."

The elderly gentleman with the cane was reading a book of poems and sipping tea. When he looked up he caught me staring and he called out, "Just ignore me! Enjoy your refreshment."

The tea was delicious, flowery and dark. After I took a few sips, I felt a funny tingle in my throat. It almost felt as if something had been unlocked inside me.

"Some people say black orchids make you tell the truth." Miss Larch had gray-green eyes that reminded me of still water. She was very calm, maybe because she was so old and had seen so much. She'd been through hurricanes and storms and harsh winters and she was still here.

"I was thinking about my father," I admitted.

"Ah, missing him, I suppose."

I went on before I could stop myself.

"I just don't understand why he would never come to visit even if he did break up with my mother."

"You think *he* broke up with *her*?"

I looked at Miss Larch carefully. She blinked and then smiled. I had the distinct impression that Miss Larch knew more about the town, and about my family, than anyone else in Sidwell.

That was part of being a historian: you collected facts and saved them up for a rainy day, or maybe simply for the day when you most needed them.

"Well, I'm not really sure what happened between them," I admitted.

"Here's my suggestion," Miss Larch said in a low voice. I felt as if I had wandered into a dream. Maybe it was the orchid tea that made me feel this way, or maybe it was simply that I'd never actually been honest with anyone outside my family before. "Don't judge your father too harshly. Not everything is what it appears to be."

I thought about what she'd said after I'd left Town Hall. I was walking past the tourist center I was writing about for my class paper. Most people passing through town would have never guessed it had been the first library in Berkshire County. Its shelves had once stored 333 books instead of maps and pamphlets, and Johnny Appleseed had planned his route across the country at one of the desks inside. Miss Larch might be right about things not being all they appeared to be. It made me think that I had to look more closely at everything I saw, and not jump to conclusions.

It was then I saw the blue painted fangs again. This time they'd been sprayed onto the side of the tourist center. Only now it wasn't just fangs; there was an entire face.

A monster crying blue tears.

YOU'LL BE SORRY IF YOU TAKE OUR HOME AWAY was scrawled in small blue letters.

A crowd had gathered round, the men of the Gossip Group among them. Some of the men were debating whether the jail cell at the police station would be strong enough to hold the monster when they caught him.

Dr. Shelton came to stand beside me. He smelled like a combination of the moss in the woods and black orchid tea. Maybe that was why I said hello.

"Remember me?" I asked.

"I certainly do. What's happening here?"

"They think a monster is writing messages and stealing things in town. They're talking about going after him."

"Miss Larch would say people need to look more carefully at what's right in front of them."

"Would she?"

I supposed they must be very good friends for him to know what she would say when she wasn't even there. Dr. Shelton was not especially tall, and he had a bit of a limp, which was why he used the cane. Now that I looked carefully, he seemed a little shabby, but he wore a clean shirt and a tie that looked somewhat familiar. I thought I might have seen Mr. Stern wearing the very same tie, and wondered if it had been among the clothes I'd overheard him say had disappeared from his laundry line. The gentleman's jacket was threadbare and he wore old hiking boots with different-colored laces, one blue and one white. But he had a nice, friendly face and bright eyes. And he was a friend of Miss Larch's, which was the best recommendation.

"Oh yes," he informed me. "She'd surely say that. And she'd be right, as usual. Why, just look at it upside down!"

Dr. Shelton smiled and walked on through the town green, whistling to himself.

I looked at the graffiti awhile longer; then I did exactly as he said. I threw down my backpack and did a handstand, even though I wasn't very good at it. Staring at the graffiti upside down, I understood that it was the face of an owl.

There was no monster. I knew that better than anyone. But now I wondered if James was responsible for the graffiti. Who would be more on the side of the owls than my brother?

I just hoped he wasn't leading people directly to him.

Sometimes I thought my mother should have listened to my grandparents. They said her decision not to remove James's wings would lead to disaster and warned that he would never know a normal life. But my mother insisted he had a right to be who he was. It was only when it came time for James to go to school that she realized how much was at stake. The reality of the danger of his situation became apparent one day in Madison Square Park in New York, while we were waiting for the swings. Two mothers on line were talking about their children's fear of monsters.

"Flying creatures scare Willy the most," we overheard one of the mothers say. "Any variety of dragons, the flying monkeys in *The Wizard of Oz,* even bats, send him screaming and searching for a place to hide."

My mother grew flushed. She patted James's head, but her expression was grim. "Don't listen," she said to him. Still, I'm sure he must have gotten an earful. I know I did.

"Why, I have to check under his bed every night with a monster light," the woman in the park went on. "That's our flashlight. I've told him that if we ever do see a monster fly by, we'll catch it in a net and bring it to the zoo. We'll lock it up and never let it out again."

We left the park and went to our favorite diner, where my mother splurged on black-and-white cookies, frosted equally in chocolate and vanilla, along with hot chocolate dotted with marshmallows. But for herself, she only ordered coffee. And she didn't even drink that. She tapped her fingertips on the tabletop and looked over her shoulder every time a new customer came through the door. That day was the end of us trying to be like everyone else.

I don't know why we left my father behind when we left New York after my grandparents' accident. But I know my mother was terribly sad. She wrote a note before we piled into the car. I remember her crying as she slipped it into an envelope. Then she did something I'll always remember. She sealed the letter with a kiss. There was a faint outline left by the pink lipstick she wore. The note was written for our father. So maybe Miss Larch had been right in asking who had left whom. My mother was the one who walked out and locked the door. I always wondered what our father thought when he came home to an empty apartment and saw the envelope on our kitchen table.

I always believed he'd come after us.

Despite everything, despite the note on the table, and the years that had passed, I still did.

Until he returned, James and I took care of each other. Whenever James sneaked out to fly, I was there waiting for him when he came back to land on the window ledge. On some nights he journeyed so far north he didn't get home until dawn, when the woods were filled with pearly light. Sometimes he tapped on the door to my room to wake me and tell me of his adventures. How the night air was filled with different constellations, how he'd rested in pastures where the cows mooed with surprise when they saw him, how he'd walked through fields of bluebells. He drank from cold springs, took to the air with owls, found caves where he would be safe when storms came up from the west.

He told me there were times when he wanted to keep on going, farther and farther north, to the edge of Canada, where no one would ever find him. In that frozen land he would hear only the echo of his own voice, and he would no longer feel like a hunted creature.

In the end, though, he always returned, his clothes torn, brambles tangled into his hair.

And now, Agate's presence made him stay closer to home.

Since the first day they'd seen each other, he'd flown over their house every night. But he had yet to try to talk to her.

"You should," I insisted. "You'd like each other."

He'd been locked away for so long, I think he didn't trust himself to speak to anyone, especially Agate.

"I wouldn't know what to say to her." I'd never seen him so unsure of himself.

"All you'd have to do is be yourself." If I was sure of anything, it was that. I'd seen the look on Agate's face when she saw him.

One day as my mother crossed the lawn, she spied James on our roof. It wasn't even dusk, but after all these years of obeying the rules, he'd become reckless. Without thinking twice, he took flight and disappeared. My mother waited on the porch for hours worrying, squinting at the sky. I crept down the stairs after midnight to discover she'd fallen asleep in the rocking chair.

In the morning, my brother landed lightly on the grass. He wore jeans and a gray sweater and his wings were folded onto his back. The wings were black, like a raven's, with stray feathers that were an iridescent blue.

Our mother woke at the sound of his footsteps. She went to embrace him, near tears. "What do you think the authorities would do if they found their monster?"

"Is that what I am?" James said softly.

"No! Of course not!" She hugged him closer. "But what will people in town think if they see you? That's why this isn't up for discussion. You have to stay home."

James moved away from her and narrowed his eyes. He was changing, becoming his own person. He'd had enough of being locked away. "I don't think I can do that," he said in a hollow voice.

I was watching from behind the old wavy-glass window set into our front door. I could tell from James's eyes, more black than gray, that he wasn't going to do as he was told anymore.

I didn't blame him.

One morning there was a knock at the door. It was Saturday and of course we weren't expecting anyone, since we never had visitors. My mother asked me to send our unexpected guest away. I thought it was probably one of those door-to-door salesmen that sometimes came through town, trying to get everyone to buy some silly product no one needed, like an umbrella for two or a folding trampoline you could carry in a suitcase or a new kind of car-wash soap that didn't need any water to do the job. I opened the door a crack. A man was pacing along the porch, talking to himself. He carried a rolled-up newspaper. When he saw me he froze.

"Hello, Twig." He was very tall and gaunt and had sad gray eyes.

"How do you know my name?" I said, suspicious.

"Doesn't everyone know everyone else in Sidwell? Isn't that what a small town is all about?" He noticed my cast and his eyes widened. "Broken?"

"A slight fracture." He still looked concerned, so I added, "I'm a fast healer. It's almost perfect already."

"That's good to know." I was about to say good-bye, adding a *Thanks but no thanks* to whatever he was selling, when he took an old-fashioned fountain pen from his pocket. Before I could stop him, he stepped forward and signed my cast. He had a very nice signature and he drew a rose at the end of his name.

"Ian Rose," he said, introducing himself. "A rose is a rose is a rose." He grinned. He had dark hair that was a little too long and somewhat shaggy. "I'm from the newspaper."

The last time I'd delivered pies to the General Store, I'd overheard the Gossip Group discuss a newspaperman from New York who had moved to town to take over as the editor of the *Sidwell Herald*. Even though he wasn't a local person, they weren't too upset that an outsider would now be in charge of Sidwell's news. He was a nephew of Miss Larch and was living in the spare bedroom of her house on Avery Street. The *Herald* wasn't much of a paper anymore, and people thought it would go out of business, but supposedly this fellow aimed to save it if he could. A few of the men made bets on the date the new editor would fail and the paper would close up shop.

"We don't want any newspapers." I began to shut the door. "Thanks anyway."

"My aunt told me to stop by. She spoke very highly of you."

"Did she?" I was flattered to hear this. I couldn't be rude to one of Miss Larch's relatives, so I kept the door open.

"She always came to New York to see me, at least once a year. I would visit occasionally when I was about your age, but I don't really know Sidwell. Now that I'm here for good, I think I'm going to feel like it's home in no time. From what I can tell, it's a nice town."

"Yes and no. It's more complicated than you would think," I said, echoing Miss Larch's sentiments.

"Most things are."

I nodded.

"I came to interview your mother," he then explained. "We could have an interesting article about the orchard in the *Herald*."

"Unlikely," I said. "She doesn't speak to strangers."

"I'm not that strange." He grinned and I grinned back.

For some reason I felt bad for Mr. Rose. Maybe because he was new to town and had no idea how unfriendly our family was. My mother was never going to talk to him. I heard a rustling in the hall. She had come to stand beside me. "Ian," she said.

I wondered if she'd met him when he'd come to town to visit Miss Larch all those years ago.

"I was just telling Twig that I'd like to write an article about the orchard."

"An article?" I expected her to send him on his way. Instead she turned to me and said, "Why don't you get some breakfast?" Then she went out to the porch, closing the door behind her.

I peered through the old glass window. When you look through it, the whole world looks very far away, almost like something in a dream. For people who didn't know each other well, my mother and Mr. Rose seemed to have a lot to say. I heard my name mentioned, which surprised me. Then I heard my mother say, "If you came to town for that, Ian, then you've made a mistake."

I must have rattled the door, because her attention shifted. When she turned to see me, she gave me a serious look that convinced me to go and get breakfast. I took out cereal and milk, but I had a funny feeling in my stomach, as if there had been an earthquake, and the ground was shifting under our feet, and everything we had ever known and been and done was about to change.

I brought James's breakfast up to the attic. Lately he hadn't been eating much, so I brought his favorite things: a bowl of cornflakes, sourdough toast, and some of our mother's homemade honey butter. The secret to the honey butter was that she added lavender, which made it so fragrant bees sometimes came in through the window to hover around the butter dish.

Mr. Rose had driven away, and my mother had begun baking strawberry pies in one of the huge ovens in the summer kitchen. We could hear her singing while she baked. The attic window was open and the air smelled like piecrust and fruit. I was glad it was Saturday and I didn't have to rush off to school. I told my brother about the graffiti, and how the artist was so smart he'd designed an image that looked like one thing right side up, and another thing altogether upside down. James looked interested, but not guilty. I could tell when he was hedging, and he wasn't. "I can't figure out who would do this," I said. "The weird thing is, there's no one who's more interested in owls than you."

"I wouldn't say that," James said. "There's the ornithologist."

So that was what Dr. Shelton did. No wonder he was always in the woods.

"You know him?"

"I've seen him recording birdsongs. I've followed him a few times. He's studying the saw-whet owls."

I couldn't quite picture Dr. Shelton with a can of spray paint, even if he was on the side of the birds.

After breakfast, James and I played Scrabble, our favorite game. I had the *X*, which made my turn difficult. There were only so many words I could think of that contained that letter. *Ox, ax, mix, exit.* None of them were worth very many points.

"Have you been over to Mourning Dove?" my brother asked.

"I can't go over there on the weekends unless I have a good excuse." I probably could have come up with one, but I was having second thoughts about my friendship with Julia. She didn't really know me; how could she like me? She'd phoned twice, and both times I'd picked up the phone, then hung up. When my mother asked who had called, I told her it had been a wrong number, someone looking for a kennel for her dog. Maybe I just wanted to end the friendship before Julia did.

James seemed to be having doubts of his own. "Agate probably thinks I was a hallucination. I'm sure she's forgotten all about me."

I didn't think so. I'd seen the look on her face. I didn't know if people really could fall in love at first sight, but if it was possible, then she had.

"I don't know how much longer I can stay in this

attic," James muttered. "I just want the same chances other people have. Is that too much to ask?"

We agreed that it wasn't. We were really very normal people, despite the wings and the curse and the way we were so solitary. I wondered if all monsters were so ordinary in their day-to-day lives, and if I should just go to the General Store and all those other places that sold T-shirts with an image of the Sidwell Monster and explain that we ate breakfast the same as they did, and that my brother was the kindest person on earth and had nothing to do with the thefts or the graffiti. Or at least, I hoped he hadn't.

"Can you help me pick out a word?" I said to Flash, who was sitting on my brother's shoulder. The little owl soared to the table. It was clear that whatever had been wrong with his wing had healed. Maybe James wasn't ready to let him go.

Flash came to peck at the *E*, which, really, was no help at all. *E* was definitely not a word in any language, not even birdspeak. Or maybe it was. I started thinking about words that began with *E*. *Excellent* and *elephant* and *ever*.

"You know you can't win against me," James teased.

"Really?" I said with a grin. "Watch." I put down *extra*, the *X* on a double-word-score space.

As I added up my score, I told James there was a new

editor at the *Sidwell Herald* who wanted to write an article about the orchard and who was Miss Larch's nephew
and seemed to know our mother, but James wasn't paying attention anymore. His eyes were fixed on what was
outside. When I went to the window, I saw why.

No one ever came to our house and now we had our
second visitor of the day. Agate was standing in the grass.
I'd been avoiding the Halls and I'd kind of forgotten how
beautiful she was. She looked like a fairy, as if she had appeared in our world by magic. Her pale hair was pulled
back and she wore a black velvet jacket over her black
dress. She was barefoot and she seemed out of breath, as
if she'd been running.

James looked at her, his changeable eyes a clear, deep
green.

Agate held something up in the air. At first I thought
it was a copy of the *Sidwell Herald* that Mr. Rose had left
behind. But it wasn't the newspaper. She was waving a
white piece of paper with a message for my brother.

Midnight at Last Lake.

My brother had a grin across his face.

He looked like any other person whose wish had
come true.

At midnight, I wasn't asleep. Old houses have noises all their own: mice in the walls, leaves hitting against the roof, footsteps on the attic floor. There was a cricket in my room, chirping away. Usually a cricket song was like a lullaby to me, but tonight it kept me awake. It was a starry night, and bright. There was a filigree of shadows on my wall from outside: tree branches, vines, and then James's shadow passing by after he went out the window. I thought of how often birds tumbled from their nests, how branches broke, how storms were the worst at this time of year, when you least expected them, when the night seemed so deep and calm. I didn't try to stop James. My heart lifted to know he was free, at least for a little while. Still, I worried. I knew my mother would be convinced that of all the people in the world, the last person James should be meeting at midnight was Agate Early Hall.

CHAPTER FOUR

The Summer That Wasn't
Like Other Summers

SCHOOL LET OUT THE FOLLOWING WEEK.
On the last day, after the books had been turned in and
the lockers cleared out, I was walking home alone, wondering what I would do all summer. The weeks stretched
out in front of me like blank pieces of paper, with the
future unwritten. I heard someone shout my name. I
turned to look behind me. Julia. It was impossible to run
away, so I stood there, nervous, while she raced over.

"Where've you been?" Julia was a little out of breath.

"Nowhere," I said blankly. "Here."

I just didn't see how a friendship could work out, so

what was the point? I had made the decision to stick with life as I knew it, which meant I was alone. But at least I wasn't dumped or betrayed.

I continued walking, and Julia did, too. It was a hot afternoon and there were bees buzzing in the fields.

"In other words, you don't want to be friends." There was a catch in Julia's voice. When I glanced at her I thought I saw a glimmer of tears in her eyes.

"*You* don't want to be friends with *me*," I corrected her.

"Who told you that? Because I never said that."

We were walking side by side, jumping into the grass whenever we heard a car behind us. It was hard having a conversation while we were either leaping around or striding along the hot blacktop.

"No one told me. I just know what will happen. Eventually you'll find other people you like better. They'll tell you I'm a nobody and you'll realize it was all a mistake, so it's just faster and easier if we're not friends from the beginning."

"Okay." Julia nodded. "Fine."

My face felt hot. This had been my fear, that it would be this easy for her to drop me. And it would hurt this much. There were probably tears in my eyes now, too.

Then Julia shocked me. "We'll be soul sisters instead. That's more than being friends. It means I won't ever think being friends is a mistake and neither will you. It means you won't guess what I'm thinking. Instead you'll talk to me and I'll talk to you, and we won't keep things from each other."

I felt a surge of relief, but I said, "We don't even have anything in common."

"Oh, like you're tall, I'm short?" Julia grinned. "Important stuff like that? Is that what you mean?"

I had to laugh. It sounded silly when she put it that way.

"We actually have tons in common," Julia went on. "We both love books, window seats, pie, dogs, and the last day of school!"

That much was true. We were walking under the tall shady trees. At this time of year in Sidwell everything was green and lush. The summer stretching out in front of me was starting to seem pretty great. Having a friend made it feel as if summer would last twice as long and be at least three times as much fun.

"And more importantly, we have a secret that binds us together," Julia said solemnly. I looked at her and she nodded. "I saw James."

Julia knew about my brother.

We went into the woods and found a quiet place where we could talk. At first I could hardly catch my breath. I didn't know how it would feel to share my secret. I didn't even know if I could share. The light coming in through the trees was yellow. There were wildflowers all around and ferns were unfolding. We'd gone pretty far, almost to the nesting place of the owls, which I could never seem to find without my brother. All the same, I had the feeling the owls were peering down at us. It was so quiet we felt we should speak in whispers, so we did. Once Julia began to talk, it was a huge relief to have someone know the truth.

She told me that one night she'd heard Agate leave Mourning Dove when everyone else was in bed. She followed her out of the house, through the tall grass, into the woods. Soon she lost sight of her sister. In the dark, she felt lost and panicked. She'd heard there was a bottomless lake nearby, and was suddenly terrified that she'd fall into it, drown, and never be heard of again.

Julia made her way through the brambles, getting more and more lost as she went on. At last she heard her sister's voice, down at the shore of the lake. Agate was sitting there with my brother. Julia crouched down, hidden by a patch of thorny bushes. If she crashed back through the brambles they'd surely hear her and know she was spying. She said she felt spellbound. There were pools of moonlight in the grass and the lake looked black and was so still it seemed more like glass than like water. Agate and James were laughing and talking. Everything seemed so perfect, until James turned and Julia saw him for who he was. He seemed like he'd walked out of the pages of a fairy tale, a mythical creature who might carry her sister into the skies and never return.

Julia rushed at him.

"Leave my sister alone!"

"We're just sitting here," James assured her. "Or we were."

Agate came between them. She looped her arms around Julia. "Please be on our side." There were bright tears in her eyes. "We'll have enough people who will be against us."

"So of course I am," Julia told me as we sat whispering in the woods. "On their side, I mean."

And of course I was, too.

Since we were now officially soul sisters, we vowed to keep their secret. Julia and I made a pact that we would do whatever we could to help James and Agate this summer. And that was how we sealed our friendship.

With trust.

After that, whenever I had free time and had finished my chores I sneaked away from the orchard. There was a heat wave, and the air was crackling as the temperature hovered around ninety-five. I usually met Julia at the shore of the bottomless lake she had blundered upon in the dark on the night she first saw James. The lake sat right between our properties. People called it Last Lake because it really was the last lake in Sidwell. All the others had dried up years ago during a heat wave that lasted all summer long, when there wasn't a drop of rain. It was said that the fish in all those other lakes grew feet and walked across the meadows and ended up in Last Lake. There certainly were a lot of fish here. We lingered by the shore so we could see their silver and blue shadows flashing below the surface of the water. There were nearly as many frogs in the shallows, where lily pads floated. Some water lily flowers were white and some were yellow and some were the palest pink. Dragonflies darted above the water, their iridescent wings catching the glint of the sunlight.

I couldn't swim because of my cast, but I could still call out "Polo" every time Julia called out "Marco" as she splashed around in the water. Afterward we would lie out on the wooden dock that my grandfather had used for fishing. We read our books out there, and wore water lilies in our hair, and we talked about the future, when we would share an apartment in New York City.

And then on one perfectly perfect day I saw it again. On a rock beside Last Lake.

The blue graffiti.

Julia hadn't shown up yet, so I turned and did a head-stand and there it was again. The face of an owl.

Julia and I were meeting at the dock so early in the morning there wasn't another soul around. It was the best time of the day. Even the frogs were still asleep. A few sparrows rustled in the bushes and doves were cooing nearby when Julia arrived. She spied the blue paint right away.

"What is that?"

We sat on the dock and I told Julia everything, how the blue monster was an owl turned upside down, how a very smart old gentleman had said it might not be what it appeared to be, how upset people were that someone was stealing from houses and stores, leaving the mark of a monster all over town.

"We have graffiti in Brooklyn and it's no big deal. It's part of New York. A lot of people think it's art."

"Well, we don't have it in Sidwell," I said. "And this graffiti seems like it's definitely a message, except I have no idea what it means."

"I'd guess someone's playing a joke. Someone who's seen too many scary movies and believes all that nonsense about the Sidwell Monster."

"If the thefts and graffiti don't stop they'll hunt down the monster. And if they find James, it's all over. They'll blame him for everything."

"We could protect him if we found the real culprit," Julia suggested.

It was a perfect idea. We immediately made a list of steps we should take:

One: Check out the spray-paint section of the hardware store.

Two: Talk to Dr. Shelton.

Three (and this was a little scary, but maybe it was how things were done in Brooklyn because it was Julia's idea): Meet the culprit.

In the meantime, we would help Agate and James and act as go-betweens. They had begun to write to each other, like star-crossed lovers in an old book. Sometimes Julia gave me a letter from her sister to bring to James. Agate used old-fashioned notepaper, the kind I didn't even think they made anymore, a creamy-white parchment. There was a gold bee imprinted on the back of the envelope. Other times I had a note from James for Julia to bring home to Agate. He used the lined paper and thin blue envelopes that I'd found in my mother's desk. It turned out my mother had quite a lot of stationery and stamps, as if she was having a long correspondence with someone, not that I'd ever seen her writing to anyone, nor had she ever received any personal mail. It was all flyers and bills, and now the *Sidwell Herald* arrived every day.

When I carried my brother's messages for Agate, I could almost read what he wrote through the sealed envelopes, but not quite.

Julia and I grinned at each other when we exchanged these love letters, but we also shivered, and not from dipping our toes in the ice-cold lake. We both had the feeling something could go terribly wrong. Wasn't that what had happened to Agnes Early and my four-times-great-grandfather Lowell? First love that had been cursed?

We planned to find out more about Agnes and Lowell

and to catch the graffiti artist, but it was summer and we had so many other things to do, the kind of things you can only do when school is over and time stretches out before you. We rode our bikes everywhere and visited every ice cream stand in Sidwell—there were four—and decided on our favorite flavors. Julia's was peppermint stick, and mine, of course, was apple cinnamon. On rainy afternoons, we sprawled out on the window seat in Julia's room to read. I was in the middle of Andrew Lang's *Red Book of Fairy Tales* and Julia had chosen the *Violet Book*. We found an old cookbook from 1900 in the pantry and on some days we took over the kitchen of Mourning Dove Cottage, making desserts that probably hadn't been made in Sidwell in a hundred years: graham cracker muffins, banana trifle, orange meringue. We collected wildflowers and pressed them between sheets of waxed paper, and thought of the poet Emily Dickinson as we did so. We painted our nails in shades we chose because of their names: First Light (silvery pearl), Saturday Night (bright red), Picnic (minty green), Summer (a delicate blue that was the color of the sky in July was my personal favorite, even though anything blue made me think of the graffiti).

One day when we were walking through town we found ourselves right in front of Hoverman's Hardware

Store. Julia and I looked at each other and we both said, "Spray paint" at the very same time. We were ready to take the first step on our list.

When we went inside a little bell over the door jingled. Usually I thought it was a pretty sound, like a fairy flitting over our heads, but now I nearly jumped out of my shoes. Julia looked a little nervous as well. When you set out to find the answers to your questions, you have to be prepared to be surprised by what you discover.

We went over to the paint section and looked around. I loved the names of the colors. Some of them were as good as our nail polish shades. Julia and I argued over which ones were the best: There was Ice Cream (I pictured vanilla, Julia said it might easily be strawberry) and Bananarama (pale yellow, of course—we both agreed on that) and Have a Heart (Red for love? Green for jealousy? We settled on pink for true love) and Butterfly (I voted for orange, like a monarch butterfly. Julia suggested pale green, like the wings of a cabbage moth). For a while I wandered off and got stuck in the blues: Aquamania, Seascape, Blue Moon, Blue Heron, Bluebell.

Julia came to guide me away. "The spray paints aren't here. I've looked everywhere. It's like they disappeared."

I finally spied them and pointed upward. The aerosol paints had been piled onto a high shelf and locked up behind wire meshing. The elder Mr. Hoverman came by, carrying some shovels. Even Miss Larch would have described him as ancient. "Under lock and key," he said of the paints we were gazing at.

"Why's that?" I asked.

"Graffiti around town. I was asked by the mayor to write down the name and address of everyone who buys any. They've got to sign their names in my book; then I get my key and let them have what they want."

"Do you remember who bought spray paint before you had to lock it up?" Julia asked.

"You girls are as bad as the sheriff with all of your questions. My memory's mostly gone, but I'll tell you what I told him: Mark Donlan, who was painting his patio furniture. Helen Carter, who had an old bike she wanted to paint. A girl who said she was going to paint silver stars."

Julia and I grinned at each other. That had been Julia, for her ceiling.

"And some boy I never saw before. About your age," Mr. Hoverman said.

Julia and I exchanged a look.

"Do you remember what he looked like?" I asked. "Or anything about him?"

"I barely remember what I look like," Mr. Hoverman

joked. At least, I thought it was a joke. He was nearly at the century mark, and he had met and seen a lot of people in his time. "Whoever he was, you can be sure he won't be getting any more paint without signing his name in my book."

It really wasn't much help to know that the culprit was a boy our age. We couldn't go around questioning everyone who fit that description. Clues were funny things. Some of them were useful and some of them weren't and some came when you least expected them.

We finally found a clue in the cellar of Mourning Dove one drizzly afternoon when we were exploring the cottage, looking for more old cookbooks. We pushed open a heavy storeroom door and there it was, as if it had been waiting politely for us to find it all this time. In the beam of our flashlight we spied something white on the ground, near a coal bin that hadn't been used in decades. It was a crinkly, translucent piece of paper. The edges were yellow and we were afraid the paper might fall into shreds if we held it for too long.

Cellars are strange places, where people tuck away bits and pieces of the past, but the last thing we expected was to find a message. Clearly, no one had been down here for years, unless you counted spiders. There were dozens of them.

We held up the flashlight and began to read.

What begins one way must end the same way.

The letters *AE* were scrawled beneath this line.

"Agnes must have written this," Julia said.

It had to be part of the enchantment.

"Maybe she'd had second thoughts about the curse," I said, "and wanted to make sure there was a way to end it." We studied the line she'd written, and finally it hit me. To undo a spell you needed to re-create it; then it would unwind, like a spool of thread.

"We have to find out exactly what she did."

We shook hands and agreed.

We would end the curse the way it had begun.

We decided to tell Agate our plans and reveal all we knew about our families' histories. She had a job as a counselor at the summer camp at Town Hall and had been put in charge of the costumes for the play. We waited for her at the end of the day. The bell in the tower of the building rang every evening at six. It was so loud it could be heard all over town, even up in the mountains, if you listened carefully. When I walked through the apple orchard and heard the ringing in the distance, the sound made me happy to live in Sidwell, where people cared about old-fashioned things like libraries and bell towers and there was someone like Miss Larch who was making sure our history wasn't forgotten.

"Fancy meeting you two here," Agate said cheerfully when she saw us. She had bits of thread and ribbon stuck to her clothes.

"It's a small town," I said.

"And you're the best sister in it," Julia added, picking a stray pin from Agate's sleeve.

"I'm getting suspicious." Agate laughed. "You either want something from me or you have bad news."

It was actually a bit of both.

We walked through town, arm in arm.

"What do you think about the play?" Julia asked her sister.

"Don't you hate the way the witch is treated?" I piped up.

"It's just a play." Agate shrugged. She'd clearly been paying more attention to the costumes than to the plot.

"But this one is special," Julia informed her sister. "She's our witch."

We sat Agate down on a bench in the park across

from the tourist center and told her everything we knew: how Agnes Early had been in love, and how she'd been betrayed. The result was the curse that had affected my brother.

"I don't believe in curses," Agate said. "That's like believing in monsters."

"Or boys with wings?" I said.

There was silence then. I'd made my point. What happened in Sidwell didn't happen in other places. Julia had told me Agate had begged my brother to take her flying, but he'd refused. He wanted to be just another normal person, the boy who walked across the orchard to meet her. But in Sidwell, things worked differently, and life wasn't what you always wanted it to be.

"We don't know what happened to Agnes or Lowell, but we plan to find out. All we know is that the curse is still with us," I went on, once the truth had sunk in. "That's why my mother was so upset when your family moved next door. She was afraid it would happen again."

"And if it does, it will all be my fault," Agate said sorrowfully.

She took off, racing across the green. We sprinted after her. Luckily I was fast enough to reach her before she could get away.

"It definitely wouldn't be your fault," I told her.

Julia had reached us, and was doing her best to catch her breath. "In the first place, it happened over two hundred years ago," she said.

"In the second place, we're going to fix it," I told Agate.

"What begins one way must end the same way," Julia and I said at the very same time.

Agate gave us both a hug. "I'll make the witch's costume the best one. She's our witch, after all."

Agate worked late at the camp after that, taking special care with the witch's costume. When she came home she often fell asleep curled up on the couch.

"How can she be so beautiful and still be so kind-hearted?" I asked. Sixteen was totally different from twelve.

"She just is," Julia said proudly. "Always has been and always will be."

No wonder my brother was under her spell. It was said that the first Agnes Early had enchanted my four-times-great-grandfather with her kindness and her beauty. Now the same thing seemed to be happening again. James left home earlier each evening, sometimes before dusk. He simply walked out the front door and walked through the orchard, like an ordinary boy, then met Agate by an old stone wall where they held hands like any other young couple. James was avoiding the attic, gone most of the time. I tried to feed his little owl, Flash, bits of hamburger and dry toast, but he wouldn't eat when James wasn't there. He waited by the window, gazing out.

One morning when I went to get our copy of the *Sidwell Herald* I noticed that someone had written in very small letters on our back door. I felt dizzy, so I sat down. I was eye-to-eye with the message. There was the word *Help*, along with a small set of fangs. I ran to the garage and got an old can of green paint and quickly painted over it. As I did so, I had to wonder: Was someone actually asking for my help? Or did they simply want to set suspicion upon my brother?

I couldn't stop thinking about the message. Every time I passed the door I could see the shadow of the words under the green paint and I thought about whoever it was who might need me to be on their side.

People in town seemed more upset about sightings of the Sidwell Monster than they were about the possibility of the woods being cut down. The Gossip Group began to have meetings at Town Hall in the evenings. Soon people outside the group started to attend. I even saw Mrs. Farrell, my English teacher, come out of a meeting with some of her friends.

"Hi there, Twig." She waved.

"Are you going to these monster meetings?" I asked. When we'd discussed *Wuthering Heights,* Mrs. Farrell told me that no man was a monster, not even Heathcliff, and that most people's misdeeds were rooted in the treatment they'd received in the world.

"Well, I'm not one to believe in such things, but something scared the life out of Emily Brontë," she said of her beloved cat. "Now she won't go into the yard." When she saw the worried look on my face she added, "We all just want Sidwell to be safe."

The *Sidwell Herald* was looking much better since Mr. Rose had taken over. Now there was a crossword puzzle and a horoscope, and a book review section, with most of the reviews written by Miss Larch, a true book lover. But my heart sank when I read the police log that night. Usually the log was filled with mentions of missing dogs, cars broken down, and lost keys and wallets. But there was one item that stopped me cold. Tourists from Boston had driven into a ditch after entering the town limits and were still in shock when the police came. After they were given bottles of cold water and some time to recover, the tourists reported spying a winged creature flying above them, and sheer terror had caused them to go off the road. They were so upset, they refused an offer of complimentary Sidwell Monster T-shirts and a free dinner at the Starline Diner.

Every day there were more reports. A truck driver spied what he said was a dinosaur, or maybe it was a hawk. Sally Ann said some sort of creature had been sitting on the roof of the diner, leaving shreds of crumpled blue paper behind. Some children at Last Lake looked up after swimming, screamed, dropped their towels, and ran home to report to their parents that a huge hawk as big as a man had frightened them away. When Sheriff Jackson went to explore he found two shimmery blue-black feathers on the shore. The feathers had been reviewed by the entire police force, three officers and a secretary, Mrs. Hardy, before being placed on display in the Sidwell history room under Miss Larch's care.

I went to see them for myself. It was lunchtime and Miss Larch was having a selection of cucumber and lettuce sandwiches with her ornithologist friend. It was the perfect opportunity for me to complete step two of our plan: Question Dr. Shelton.

Miss Larch poured us White Dragon tea, which she said gave the drinker courage and an open heart. When she went to get the sugar bowl and some napkins, I sat down beside Dr. Shelton. He still smelled a little mossy, like he'd just been trekking through the woods. He seemed to prefer the cucumber sandwiches to the lettuce ones. I tried one and was surprised to find it was delicious. I thought I might fix all sorts of vegetable sandwiches this summer: tomato and butter, asparagus and cream cheese, green beans and peanut butter.

"What do you think of all this talk about a monster?" I asked, just to get a sense of Dr. Shelton's thinking.

"Stuff and nonsense," he said.

"What about the graffiti?"

"*Don't take our home away* plus the face of an owl. If you put it together what do you get . . . ?"

I suddenly understood what it meant. "The owl nesting area! That's their home."

"That's what I would presume if I were presuming things." Dr. Shelton looked so proud of me I felt as if I were an A student.

"Does someone want to take the owls' home?"

"Sometimes the most important part of research is

asking the right question. I think you would make an excellent researcher. Most likely, quite a bit better than most of the scientists at the university who'll examine the new exhibit." Dr. Shelton nodded to the glass case.

"Scientists?" I didn't like the sound of that.

"The ones who will test the feathers for their DNA."

I thought this over while we had our tea and came to a decision. Maybe there was something to the White Dragon tea's effects. I did feel as if I had more courage.

I thanked Miss Larch for lunch, then headed toward the door. I stopped at the case where the feathers were displayed, set onto some draped blue fabric. I looked over my shoulder and saw Miss Larch tidying up the cups and plates, so I opened the case, slowly, making certain it wouldn't creak. I slipped the feathers into my cast.

I glanced up and for a minute I thought Dr. Shelton was watching me, but I couldn't be sure. I walked out, casually, as if I had nothing to hide, even though my heart was pounding. Then I ran home as fast as I could.

I could barely sleep that night. I'd never stolen anything before, although technically it wasn't stealing if you were taking something that belonged to your own family. All the same, I felt like I'd committed the crime of feather theft. And I felt especially bad when I considered what Miss Larch would think when she saw they were missing. I finally fell asleep, but when I woke up in the middle of the night, I thought the moon was a police car headlight.

The next day I grabbed the newspaper, looking for a story about the history room theft at Town Hall, figuring it would be a front-page article since not much news happened here. But the missing feathers were only mentioned briefly on the next-to-last page, right below a story about a lost cat named Jitters. I was pleased to see that Mr. Rose had written an editorial about the importance of the Montgomery Woods to the town of Sidwell.

I went to Julia's to tell her about Dr. Shelton, and how I'd realized that the graffiti message had something to do with the nesting owls.

"If it's someone on the side of the owls," Julia said thoughtfully, "then he can't be all bad."

I didn't say anything, but all that day as we finished up the stars on her bedroom ceiling, I wondered if James was behind the graffiti messages. He had shown me the nesting area, and I'd seen for myself how baby owlets would come to perch on his shoulders.

We'd just finished the last star on the bedroom

ceiling when Mrs. Hall came upstairs with a rolled-up sheet of paper. It looked very old and dusty.

"Look at this, girls," she said, excited. "Here are the plans for the original garden."

Mrs. Hall had found the old document on the top shelf of the library, hidden beneath some maps of Sidwell. She told us it appeared to be a colonial herb garden set out where a tangle of weeds now grew. The plan included four gravel walkways that met in the middle with a circle of stones that surrounded a wildflower garden. Printed in curly letters was the phrase *Have the garden near the dwelling, for beauty and ornament, and most of all for reason.* There was a list of herbs that had been used: tansy, parsley, sage, bayberry, thyme, lavender, rosemary, mint, yarrow, wormwood, and feverfew.

Dr. Hall came in from the hospital. After looking over the garden plan, he explained that many of the herbs were used for their medicinal value. "Some are still used today. If you have a stomachache, eat parsley. If you're nervous, rest your head on a pillow of lavender." That explained why I felt so relaxed after eating the lavender honey butter my mother made. Even a rose had a purpose, the doctor told us, for the petals and rose hips could be made into a soothing tea. I had the feeling that re-creating Agnes Early's garden was a part of the spell.

What begins one way must end the same way.

It was the beginning of setting things right. It was what we were meant to do.

Julia and I got permission to begin work right away. Dr. Hall drove us out to the garden center on Milldam Road and we both used our savings to buy as many plants as we could. The owner of the garden center, Mr. Hopper, threw in some wilted plants for free when he heard about our endeavor. "Just so long as you know it's a witch's garden you're planning," he said as he helped us load up the car.

"That's fine," Julia said. "We like witches."

"We think they've been unjustly persecuted," I added.

I spied Mr. Rose at the cash register. He was buying a rosebush with enormous blooms, pink with creamy-yellow centers. They were lemony and rosy and fragrant. Mr. Rose waved a hello and I waved back. I didn't mean to like him, but for some reason I did.

"I read your editorial," I called as we headed to the parking lot.

"Approve or disapprove?" he called back.

"Oh, approve. Most definitely."

Just as I approved of his choice of roses.

Julia and I worked in the garden every chance we had. It was difficult for me to use one arm, but I did the best I could, and I got pretty good at digging and planting with one hand. If my mother ever wondered where I was, she never mentioned it. In the summers before the Halls arrived, I'd spent most of my time in the orchard, and I assumed that was where she figured me to be. She loved gardens, so I didn't think she would be upset if she learned I was helping to create one.

Dr. Hall helped us turn the earth with a shovel and he made the gravel paths that cut the garden into four equal sections, following Agnes Early's plan. He said clearing the garden cleared his head from doctoring. It was hot, dirty work, but none of us minded. The birds seemed especially interested in what we were doing once the planting began and often gathered around to watch, or to pick out the worms from the turned earth. Slowly, the garden came back to life. I had the feeling that Agnes Early would have been happy to see it this way. That maybe her broken heart would have begun to heal.

One afternoon when I went to the General Store to buy flour and sugar for my mother, I overheard the Gossip Group discussing recent events in town. One of them said if he ever did see the Sidwell Monster he'd take a shot and wouldn't miss. Before I could think better of it I blurted out, "You just want to kill things!"

"Wait a minute, Twig," Mr. Stern called after me. "Not everyone feels that way!"

But it was too late. I'd begun to run for the door. I slammed out of the store, even though Mr. Stern had always been so nice when I brought pies and cider for him to sell.

I ran all the way home. Now that I'd overheard the conversation in the General Store, I understood why James refused whenever Agate begged him to take her flying. It was far too dangerous, and he'd begun to rethink their spending time together.

Maybe he'd been right to believe his fate was to be alone in the air and on earth.

I could hardly wait for us to right whatever had gone wrong so long ago. We worked in the garden every day. The more plants we put in, the more birds gathered to sing to us. When Agate came to help us weed, we discovered she could call the mourning doves to her. "James taught me." A worried look crossed her face. "Do you have a letter for me?" she asked then. I hated that I had to tell her no. "I didn't think so. He's not coming to meet me anymore," she told me. "I don't know why."

"He thinks he's putting you in harm's way when he meets you."

"Shouldn't that be my decision?" Agate said.

I didn't know the answer to that. I only knew that the curse had hurt too many people.

When we'd planted all the herbs, we stood there holding hands. We were that much closer to completing our mission. The doves flew around us, calling in their soft voices. It was almost as if Agnes Early was with us, giving her permission for us to go on. The air crackled with heat and magic.

Something had begun.

To create the wild garden in the center of the circle, we went into the woods and found lady slippers and ferns, wild asters and little blue flowers in the shape of stars. Sometimes I went out into the woods after dusk, searching for night-blooming flowers. One evening as I walked home in the dark I thought I heard something rattling around in the thickets. Probably a raccoon or some squirrels. All the same I felt goose bumps rise on my arms, even though I'd walked through these woods my whole life. It was then I saw a flash of silver. A spray-paint can. Someone was here in the woods. I spied the shadow of a boy as he ducked behind a tree. He looked about my age, and he was dressed in black. All at once I heard a siren. A car with bright headlights and a flashing red light came up behind me on the path. It was Sheriff Jackson.

"Twig," the sheriff called. "What are you doing wandering around in the dark?"

I blinked. I had actually caught the graffiti artist in the act, but I didn't want to turn him in until I understood why he was pretending to be the Sidwell Monster. "I'm going home for dinner," I stammered.

"Through the woods? You wouldn't want to run into the monster, would you? This is near the place where those feathers were found. They've disappeared from Town Hall. Someone around here is not to be trusted," the sheriff said.

"I'll be careful," I told him, my heart beating fast.

"Okay," he said. "Go straight home."

The car pulled away, but I stood still. I spoke into the darkness. "I won't turn you in. I just want to know who you are."

There was no reply.

"I want to help you," I said to the woods around me.

When I got home my mother was waiting for me on the porch. I told her about the graffiti, and how everyone thought the monster was behind it, and how Sheriff Jackson had been driving through the woods searching for whoever was to blame.

My mother put an arm around my shoulders. "Now that they're looking for someone they may find James. I don't know what will happen if they do."

My mother usually didn't confide her worries. She always wanted to seem strong, but now her face was pale and I thought she'd been crying.

"There must be a cure for every curse," I told her with assurance. I'd read that somewhere, in a nursery rhyme.

"Oh, Twig," my mother said. "The time for a cure has passed."

"But maybe there's another cure, one no one knows about." I wasn't ready to tell her about my plans with Julia to undo Agnes Early's spell. Not until I was sure it would work.

"I wish there was." My mother seemed more open to talking than usual. We could see fireflies from our porch. It seemed as if anything could happen, if we just believed it could.

"What else do you wish for?" My mother usually clammed up when I asked anything too personal. Maybe it made her too sad. Maybe she wished that things had turned out differently and we could have more of the sort of life other people had.

"I wish I could go back in time," my mother said.

I imagined she wanted to break the curse. "To two hundred years ago?"

She laughed. "No. Not that far back. I can't see myself living in the days when there were witches and curses. I'd just like to go back to when we lived in New York City."

That was the time when we tried our best to be ordinary people, when the future seemed as if it might be happy. When my father was there.

"Let's count fireflies," my mother said.

It was an old game with us and we reached two

thousand before we gave up. There was so much light in the world we knew we would never be able to count it all.

The next day I helped with the baking out in the summer kitchen. I felt closer to my mother now that we'd talked. We both wanted the same thing: for James to be safe. My mother took the time to teach me how to make piecrust, which is harder than you'd guess. The best kind is made with ice water and very pure flour. Then she told me the secret of Pink apple pie. She whispered that the ingredient that made it so sweet was jam made from our own strawberries and raspberries, but she made me promise never to tell anyone other than my own daughter one day.

I left the summer kitchen while my mother was waiting for the last of the pies to finish baking. It was such a perfect July afternoon I couldn't imagine living anywhere other than Sidwell. I loved the orchard that was filled with green shadows, and the gold light filtering through the woods. I didn't remember too much about New York, although my brother had often described the great avenues and the silver buildings and our tiny apartment that overlooked the river.

I was thinking about New York City, how I'd like to visit there someday, just to experience it, and go to a theater and see a real play, not just one about the Witch of Sidwell, when I noticed something beside the porch. It was bundled up in burlap. I couldn't quite make out what it was, but I could pick up the scent from a distance: the lemon-drop fragrance of the special roses from the garden center.

Mr. Rose had been to our house. I didn't say anything about the gift he had left for my mother, but it made me like him even more. Other women would have preferred a box full of long-stemmed roses, but my mother liked more old-fashioned things, teacup-sized blooms she could grow for years to come. Mr. Rose seemed to know that about her.

In the morning I was surprised when I found the rosebush beside the trash barrel. Maybe Mr. Rose should have knocked on the door and given his gift directly to my mother, but I understood what it was like to be shy. I decided to take the rosebush with me to Julia's, though I had to struggle to carry it. When we planted it in the witch's garden the scent of the flowers was like lemons and cherry tarts and Pink apple pie all mixed together in one delicious breath.

"They're perfect," Julia said. And they were.

Summer was moving too quickly. It was already the end of July, time for me to have my cast taken off at the hospital. I was nervous, but it didn't hurt. My cast arm was much paler and it was a bit stiff, but every day it felt a little stronger. It was so wonderful to have both of my arms again that I danced in the grass and climbed a tree, more carefully this time; then Julia and I celebrated by swimming in Last Lake. Swimming had never been as wonderful or as cold and refreshing. So far it had been an exceptionally good summer. I had a best friend and we had finished planting the herb garden and I had learned to make a piecrust and I knew the secret of Pink apple pies. But I still couldn't sleep at night, not until I heard James come home. Sometimes he sat out on the roof. I wondered if anyone had ever felt as alone as he did. Flash, the little owl, had healed and had relearned how to fly. Now he went with my brother on his journeys into the woods. The little owl could have remained there, but he always returned when my brother did, at the hour when all the other birds were waking. Many of those James had saved came back to perch in the branches of the trees. It was heartwarming to see the trust they had in him.

James stayed out on the roof in the first rays of daylight. He was gazing north, into the treetops, toward the mountains, where he could be free. He didn't have to tell me what he was planning. Sooner or later there would come a morning when he didn't come back.

I knew how he felt about the peace that could be found in the woods. When I went there alone I always felt comforted by the sound of birdsongs and the deep greenery. I wanted to find the place where the saw-whet owls nested, but it was so deep in the woods and so hidden, I never could find that place my brother had taken me to. And then one day I saw blue letters spray-painted on a rock.

FOLLOW.

My heart thudded against my ribs.

I continued walking; then I realized I had entered the owl nesting area. I kept on and saw paint on another rock. This one said *LOOK UP.*

There in the tree above me was a rustic tree house, a simple shelter made of a wooden platform covered by a shingled roof. Sitting there was Miss Larch's friend. No wonder Dr. Shelton smelled mossy; he was living in a tree.

"Hello," I called up.

He was startled and grabbed a broom, I suppose to protect himself. Then he said, "Twig." He nodded as if he had been expecting me, and I felt a little flattered that he remembered me at all.

"Don't stumble around," he said. "Come up."

He tossed down a rope ladder. For about half a second I hesitated. Then I climbed up. He had a bedroll and a desk and a bookcase made of branches.

"You're a good climber," he said.

I took it as a serious compliment. "That's why I'm called Twig."

Dr. Shelton had a collection of binoculars and notebooks. The desk was covered with feathers. I thought I recognized his quilt as one my mother had hung up on our laundry line to dry in the sun.

"Someone left me a message for me to find you," I said.

I more than suspected that he was the thief the Gossip Group talked about.

"Do you mind if I ask what you're doing up here?" I asked.

Miss Larch's friend reached into his jacket pocket for his card. He was a *Professor of Ornithology, Retired, PhD Cornell University.* Under his name was written *The Owl Man.* "My specialty."

"The black saw-whet owls." Exactly as my brother had told me.

He nodded. "If I can prove they are specific to this area and that they will face extinction if construction begins, then I may be able to stop the ruination of these woods."

"Are you writing the graffiti?"

"No. But I can't say I'm against it. The writer is on the side of these woods."

"Is it the same person who brought you the quilt?"

"If he did, then he's generous," Dr. Shelton said. "If I told you any more I would be an ungrateful wretch."

"He's generous with other people's belongings." The fact was, the quilt was an old one and we didn't miss it very much, and I really didn't mind Dr. Shelton using it, since he needed it more than we did.

"If I'm correct in my thinking, then I would say he's even more generous with his own. What belongs to him, he wants to give to all of Sidwell."

As I walked home I thought it was best not to judge what I didn't understand. But that didn't mean I would stop trying to get to the bottom of the secrets of Sidwell.

CHAPTER FIVE

The Message
and the Messenger

JULIA FOUND THE DIARY WHEN SHE WASN'T expecting to stumble upon it. This seemed to be the way enchantments worked, appearing when you least expected them to. All the best things happen that way, on an ordinary day that's like any other until everything suddenly changes. Julia was in the library, which was the oldest part of Mourning Dove Cottage, where the bookshelves were filled with dusty, timeworn volumes about things like cheese making and table manners. There was a small mahogany writing desk in the corner. It wasn't the nicest piece of furniture; in fact, it was ugly, with shaky bowed legs and drawers that stuck shut and refused to open in damp weather. The desk seemed as if it might fall apart if you breathed on it too hard. Mrs. Hall had been thinking about bringing it down to Blue Door Antiques on Main Street to see if they might like to try to sell it.

Julia wanted to send a postcard with a photograph of Sidwell to her cousin in England. She opened a drawer to look for a pen. When she reached inside she felt a latch at the back. She slipped it up, to find a hidden space. Inside was a small leather-bound book. Agnes Early's diary.

It seemed only fitting that if we wanted to undo the curse we should read the diary in the herb garden. Julia phoned me and I ran all the way. She waited to turn the first page until we were sitting in the shade of a tangle of roses that were now in full bloom. Bees were humming all around us. We were ready to step back in time, my mother's wish and my wish now, too.

What begins one way must end the same way.

I read the first line aloud.

This is a place where I can write my heart.

And so she did. She wrote about my four-times-great-grandfather and his green eyes, and how she thought about him while she worked in her garden planting the same herbs that we now grew: tansy, lavender, mint. She planned the life they would have together, forever after. She and Lowell Fowler had grown up together and everyone in Sidwell knew they were fated to marry someday.

But Agnes's parents thought she was too young, and besides, war was breaking out, the American Revolution. The year was 1775. The Early family was from England, and they sided with the king. The Fowlers, on the other hand, were American through and through and had joined with George Washington's rebels to fight the king and his army of Red Coats. Families who had been friends and neighbors became enemies overnight. Aggie and Lowell were no longer allowed to see each other.

And so a secret plan was made.

We will meet by the lake on the last day of July and run away to Boston, where our families cannot find us, so that we can be married.

When Julia read that line out loud Beau began to bark. I had goose bumps up and down my arms. Crickets were calling in the tall grass. It was almost August. I knew Julia and I were both thinking the same thing: Agnes Early was probably sitting in the exact same place where we were now when she wrote down these words.

He did not come.

Agnes had waited with her packed bag. The wedding dress she'd stitched by hand, always sewn in secret when her parents were asleep, was carefully folded inside. The meeting place was the field beyond Last Lake, which was called Early Lake then, for the other lakes hadn't yet dried up. Perhaps that was part of the curse as well.

She waited all night long. But Lowell Fowler had disappeared without a sign. Agnes went to his parents, who knew nothing and were beside themselves with worry. His neighbors searched the woods and found no clues. It was as if he had never existed. His horse waited in the barn; his dog paced the meadow.

Agnes Early waited a day, a week, a month, a year.

And then, she disappeared as well. Before she left Sidwell, she made one last entry in her diary. She wrote that she had combined the herbs in the garden with two petals from the rosebush Lowell had given her as a gift, a tiny specimen that had come all the way from England by ship and had bloomed on the day he disappeared. On the night of the first full moon in August, Agnes created the spell that forever after cursed the men of our family.

Let him fly even faster from me if that's what he desires! Let him have wings!

She never wrote again.

I wandered through the woods to think things through, trying to figure out what could have made Lowell leave Agnes Early without a word. Could it be that he hadn't meant to hurt her? People often hurt the ones they love most, don't they? Without ever meaning to, they lash out, walk away, never see one another again. Or maybe it had all been beyond Lowell's control, like lightning striking him when he least expected it.

That was when I saw someone skulking about in the woods. A boy with a black backpack.

He was tall, with fair hair. He clearly knew these woods, but so did I. I started following him. I managed to stay quiet until there was a crunching sound when I stepped on a pinecone. I quickly ducked behind some bramble bushes. When he turned to glance over his shoulder, I got a good look at his face. My heart hit against my chest. He seemed familiar somehow. I should have gone back, but I guess I wasn't thinking straight. I followed him through the woods, but all of a sudden, he disappeared. I had the feeling I'd imagined him, and that I'd been tracking a shadow or some fog; then I realized he'd slipped through a black wrought-iron gate.

I'd found the back entrance to the Montgomery estate.

Unless I was very much mistaken, I'd also found the graffiti artist.

Colin Montgomery. The boy whose family owned these woods.

I noticed there was a pile of stones once used for an old road that had fallen apart. I picked out some white ones; then, as quickly as I could, I arranged them to spell out my message:

I'll help you.

I walked home slowly, thinking about how complicated families were and how many secrets people kept. Now I had one, too. One I didn't intend to mention to Julia, or even to James. I needed to figure some things out first.

I didn't realize how long I'd been gone until I stepped through our front door. There was my mother, waiting for me.

"Where have you been?" A worried expression crossed her face. "Half the time I don't even know if you're home. Is there something I should know about?"

"I've been thinking," I said.

My mother laughed. "Well, there's nothing wrong in that! What a relief!"

"I've been thinking about our family history."

My mother didn't seem so cheerful when she heard that. "I can't help you. Sorry."

She went into the kitchen, intending to end the conversation, but I followed her.

"I've been thinking about Lowell Fowler."

My mother smiled faintly. "That's ancient history."

"Seriously." I wasn't giving up. "I don't know anything about him."

My mother shrugged and told me she didn't know much either. Only that his parents had begun this orchard and our family had been here ever since. He'd lived and died in Sidwell.

"Did he disappear?" I wanted to know.

"Into the woods to think?" she teased.

"Mom. Seriously."

"If he did disappear, he came back. He's buried in the town cemetery." My mother was distracted, turning the pages of the *Sidwell Herald*.

I started for my room but found James in the hallway, headed toward the front door. "Don't try to stop me," he told me. "I can't live this way anymore."

"If Julia and I figure out the cure you won't have to. If we can find out what happened to Lowell, maybe we can reverse it."

"Don't you think someone would have stopped it a long time ago if it could have been done?"

Instead of listening to me, James went outside to the front porch. It was a beautiful afternoon. I thought of all the days he'd been locked away. I felt a lump in my throat as I went to stand beside him. I didn't blame him for not having faith in anything. But at least he had me to back him up. The boy at the Montgomery estate seemed to have no one.

"Some nights, I don't fly," my brother told me. "I put on my long coat and I walk out the door like I'm anybody else. I head down the road and go through town. I stand on Main Street. I sit on the steps of Town Hall. I look in through the library windows. Just so I'll know what it's like to be normal. No one's caught me yet."

A car had turned onto the dirt road that led to our house. I worried it might be the sheriff again, but James didn't seem concerned.

"Maybe it's time for everyone to see me. Maybe it's fate. Let them put my picture on T-shirts so people can see the real Sidwell Monster. Here I am!" he shouted to the car.

It wasn't the sheriff, but I tugged on James's arm and dragged him inside. I had recognized Mr. Rose's car, and if James wasn't quick his story might be plastered all across the front page of the *Herald*.

"Just for now," I said. "Stay inside."

When Mr. Rose got out of his car I was back out on the porch, sitting on the railing. He handed me the quart of ice cream he'd brought along. I checked out the flavor. Apple cinnamon. My favorite. I looked at him carefully, wondering if he was a mind reader or if he just happened to have the same taste as me.

"Hello, Twig. I could have sworn someone was standing here with you."

"Nope," I said, my fingers crossed behind my back. "Just me and my shadow."

"Funny," he mused. "I have twenty-twenty vision. Is your shadow a tall boy, about four years older than you?"

I shook my head, feeling panic rising. Could it be that he really was a mind reader? "Maybe you should get your eyes checked. Vision changes as you age."

"You're right. I probably should."

I hadn't heard my mother come up behind me, but suddenly there she was. "Teresa," she said, using my given name for emphasis. "Why don't you put that ice cream in the freezer. I'm going to have a talk with Mr. Rose."

I was stunned. I would have never expected her to go walking through the orchard with a newspaper editor when we had so much to hide and so much at stake if anyone found out about James. All the same, she looked so happy I felt happy, too, and when Mr. Rose waved to me from the orchard, I waved back.

Sometimes you think you know what's going to happen next, and then the world surprises you, especially in Sidwell. I went walking to think things over. I found myself back at the old gates of the Montgomery estate. I suppose I wanted to see if my message was still there. It wasn't. The stones were all scattered. At first I thought it was an accident—some deer had run by and wrecked my words. Then I realized the stones had been rearranged to form a message back to me.

Thank you Twig.

CHAPTER SIX

At the Intersection of the Past, the Present, and the Future

MY MOTHER HAD SAID LOWELL HAD BEEN buried in the Sidwell Cemetery, so that was where Julia and I went next. The old cemetery was on one of the steepest roads outside of Sidwell. It hadn't been used since 1901, when a new cemetery was built a little closer to town. We hiked up and finally made it. It was a hot day and the sky was a fragile cloud-streaked blue. The grass was so tall it reached past our knees. There were blackbirds wheeling above us, screaming at us as if we didn't belong, doing their best to chase us away.

I hadn't yet told Julia about Colin Montgomery. I

just didn't want to share him with anyone. Not yet. But whenever I kept a secret from someone it built a wall between us, and now it was happening with Julia. She chatted away, but I stayed quiet, deep in my own thoughts. It was easy enough to do. This was a place where silence felt right.

The cemetery was surrounded by a rusty iron fence. But the gate wasn't locked and was easy to push open. We put our hands against the metal, and in seconds, we were inside.

Several members of the Fowler family had been buried here, along with the ancestors of many townspeople whose names I recognized: the great-grandparents of Mr. Stern from the General Store; the aunts and uncles of the drama teacher, Mrs. Meyers; several relatives of Mr. Hopper from the garden center; even a Larch or two.

We found Lowell's grave on a hillside where there were banks of wild pink roses. It was off by itself and had the plainest of markers, a simple white stone. Julia and I crouched down so we could clear off the dust and pebbles and read the inscription.

Lowell Fowler, son of Sidwell
Now I can fly free

"He probably thought Agnes would still be here when he came back," Julia said, a sad cast in her eyes.

I nodded in agreement. "Only this time she was the one who had disappeared."

"Their true fate was interrupted."

It was always windy on this hillside, even on a bright sunny day. I had the shivers. I noticed that something had been left on Lowell's grave. A white stone. I looked around. There was nothing but grass and wild roses and the iron fence all around us.

I almost told Julia about Colin Montgomery then.

But I didn't.

She was talking about what we needed to do next. "I'll search the cottage to see if Agnes left any more clues on how to undo the spell. I'm going to find out where she went when she left Sidwell. We're going back to Brooklyn this weekend so my father can finish his work there and we can pick up some boxes we left behind. I'll go to the library and see if there's anything in their files about Agnes."

"I'll try to find out why Lowell disappeared in the first place and where he was during those missing years."

We didn't want fate to get all confused again.

While Julia was gone I went to the newspaper office on the corner of Fifth and Main. I was ready to research

Lowell Fowler, but there was someone else's life I wanted to check into as well. Mr. Rose was an editor, used to digging into stories, and for some reason I felt I could trust him. I thought he would likely understand issues of crime and destiny. Maybe he could help me figure out whether you should turn a person in when he might be doing something that could get him in trouble, something that might affect your family and maybe the whole town.

A bell rang over the door when I went inside the newspaper office. The sound was jingly, like the sleigh bells that used to hang on horse-drawn sleds. I felt as if I was stepping back in time again, and to tell the truth, it was a good feeling. The past seemed like the place where things could be settled and sorted out.

Mr. Rose was sitting behind an old-fashioned oak desk with lots of different cubbyholes filled with bills and letters. There was a computer, but he was writing longhand. He hurried to put his notepad away when he saw me. What he was writing looked a little like a love letter. I was fairly certain I saw a heart next to the rose where he'd signed his name.

"Twig!" he said cheerfully. "To what do I owe the pleasure of your company?"

I sat in a worn leather chair. For some reason the way

Mr. Rose said my name made me smile. I tried to remember to be standoffish, the way I was with everyone else in town, but it wasn't easy. "I need some information. I'm on my way to the history room at Town Hall to see Miss Larch."

"Aunt Florence." Mr. Rose nodded. "Excellent historian. No one knows more about Sidwell."

"But I also need some more current information."

"At your service." He moved his chair away from his desk and crossed his long legs, ready to listen.

There were only two other employees, Mr. Higgins and Miss Hayward, both busy on the phone. I couldn't help but overhear bits of their conversations. Mr. Higgins was talking to his daughter Ruth about dinner—he preferred fried chicken to beef stew—and Miss Hayward was speaking with her dentist's office about an appointment to have her teeth checked. Not exactly breaking news. Both reporters were about ninety years old and had worked for the paper forever. Miss Hayward wrote up the police log. Mr. Higgins covered the social scene, which included school plays, town meetings, and the apple festival. They called out to me after they finished with their phone calls.

"Fancy seeing you here, Twig," Mr. Higgins said.

"Make yourself at home," Miss Hayward said

warmly. "I'm in a forgetting state when I work, so in case I haven't said so, hello and how are you?"

I said hello back and assured Miss Hayward I was fine; then I turned to Mr. Rose. I lowered my voice. "I wanted to find out something about the Montgomery family."

"So do I. Seems like we're on the same wavelength."

Mr. Rose brought out some files.

"Mr. Montgomery bought acres of the woods bordering Sidwell twenty years ago. He lives in Boston and used to spend summers here, but in the past couple of years he's only come up occasionally."

I thought back to the summer when I was supposed to play the witch. I remembered my friend from that time. It was Colin Montgomery. That was why he'd looked so familiar at his gate. Even at five he'd been a tall, shy boy with blond hair who carried a black backpack. "Good-bye, Twig," he'd said to me on the day I had to leave and give up my part. We always had lunch together out in the playground, and because he never liked his own lunch, I always gave him half of mine. "Goodbye, Collie," I'd said. He'd grinned at me, because we'd both had nicknames.

"I've been researching Hugh Montgomery for an article," Mr. Rose went on. "He plans to develop the woods, put up a hundred houses, along with a shopping center, several restaurants, maybe even a new school. The town has to vote in September. The construction would mean jobs, so some people are for it, but it would also ruin many of the things most people in this town love most."

"The woods," I said.

Mr. Rose nodded. "The woods."

"What about the owls?" I said.

Mr. Rose leaned forward. "What owls?"

"The black saw-whet owls. They only exist in Sidwell. Miss Larch's friend Dr. Shelton knows all about them."

"Does he?" Mr. Rose shrugged on his jacket. "Why don't I walk you over to see Miss Larch?"

Because of his long legs, Mr. Rose walked fast. I had long legs, too, but I still had to hurry to keep up with him. I was a little nervous about going back to Town Hall after I'd stolen the feathers. Once we went inside, I looked over my shoulder, afraid someone would grab me and say, *"Aha, here's the thief!"* Luckily, no one noticed me as I followed Mr. Rose.

We passed the auditorium, where the camp was rehearsing the play that was always performed on August 1, the day of Lowell's disappearance.

One little girl was clearly the witch. She was dressed

all in black, standing on the papier-mâché cliff. "Do not pry into my business if you know what's best for you and yours!" she said in a shaky voice.

"I hate this play," I told Mr. Rose.

We watched as the little witch was pushed off the cliff by the other kindergartners. She fell too hard, skinned her knee, and started to cry.

"I can understand why," Mr. Rose said. "It should be rewritten."

"Someday," I assured him, "it will be."

"Someday, I plan to see your version." That made me like him even more. "Shall we delve into Sidwell history?" He opened the door to Miss Larch's domain. "Aunt Florence." Mr. Rose greeted her with a kiss on the cheek. "I've brought Twig for some historical help." His glance strayed to the table. He noticed it was set for two. "Were you expecting anyone else?"

"Well, it appears that I'm expecting Twig now, aren't I?" Miss Larch said.

I could tell she wasn't very practiced in keeping secrets.

Mr. Rose looked directly at his aunt. "I've got some research to do on owls. You couldn't help me out with that, could you?"

"I would if I could, but I can't. Owls are not my personal specialty, and what others know, I can't divulge."

I suspected Miss Larch was used to protecting Dr. Shelton and that she had her reasons, just as I had my reasons for protecting James, and now, it seemed, for protecting Colin Montgomery as well.

"I think you can trust me, Aunt Florence," Mr. Rose said. "I want what's best for Sidwell. And I think you know, I can keep a secret."

"If you do find the person who can help you," Miss Larch said, "give him this. He might be hungry. Tell him I sent you."

She cut a large slice of the cinnamon coffee cake set out on a flowered platter and wrapped it in a napkin.

"Turn left at Last Lake," she said. "Then look up."

Mr. Rose nodded, then turned to me. "Good luck, Twig. I hope you find what you're looking for."

"I hope you do, too."

We shook hands and I had a sort of teary feeling for no reason. I guess I had the sense that we were trying to save Sidwell together, even if no one knew we were trying to save the people we cared about as well.

"My nephew is a fine fellow," Miss Larch told me when we were alone. She had put up the kettle for tea.

We were having memory tea, which was especially fitting considering that my research had to do with the past. It was ginger peach with a hint of vanilla. "Heartbroken, though," Miss Larch added.

"Really?" I might have been right to guess that Mr. Rose had been writing a love letter when I first walked into the *Herald*'s office.

"You can always see heartbreak in a person's eyes. Plus he sings love songs to himself. That's a sure sign."

My mother sang love songs when she thought I couldn't hear. Actually, I noticed Miss Larch was singing a love song as she fixed our tea. *The very thought of you and I forget to do the little ordinary things that everyone ought to do.*

She had also forgotten to put out teaspoons and sugar, not that I minded. I hadn't known you could fall in love at Miss Larch's age.

"What brings you here today?" she asked.

I told her about Lowell, my four-times-great-grandfather, and how he'd disappeared in 1775 and left heartbreak behind and no one seemed to know why.

"It was the beginning of the American Revolution," Miss Larch said as she went to the files. "The shot heard round the world was fired in Concord, and that was the beginning of our country. Unfortunately, if you're looking for the news from that time, there may be a problem. There was a major fire in Sidwell soon after. Lightning struck and started the sparks. Half of Main Street was burned down.

"I have seen some papers on Lowell Fowler. He was a war hero. There was a grand parade for him on Main Street when he returned. Biggest one Sidwell's ever had. And then Johnny Chapman, better known as Johnny Appleseed, gave him the Pink apple tree and the orchard began."

Miss Larch put on her reading glasses, then took out the records from the year Lowell went missing. Thankfully Town Hall hadn't burned down in the fire and there was still an accounting of marriages, births, deaths, and military records, dating back to the 1700s.

On the evening of July 31, 1775, all able-bodied young men left Sidwell to fight the British. The information was common knowledge; it was all written up in the pamphlet tourists were given when they visited Sidwell. But there was more that no one knew. After all the men had gathered, one was missing: Lowell Fowler.

When the other men in town went to search for him, they found him walking in the woods on his way to meet Aggie Early. He told them he couldn't go to Concord, even though he was a patriot. He explained the next day was to be his wedding day and a man couldn't miss that, even for a war against the king. But the men of Sidwell wouldn't listen. They insisted that it was every patriot's duty to go to fight, even the ones in love. The war wouldn't wait and that was that.

They took him without a minute to say good-bye.

That was the minute that changed his fate and ours.

Lowell proved his courage, saving many of his friends during his year in service, including several citizens of Sidwell, one of them a relative of Miss Larch's.

"Think of that! I wouldn't exist without him and neither would Ian!" Miss Larch said. "You'd be sitting here talking to an empty chair. As a matter of fact, a lot of us wouldn't be here if not for Lowell Fowler!"

"Could he have written any letter back home?"

"Likely not. The mail and everything else had been disrupted. War is war, and letters, even if written, are easily misplaced."

After the war Lowell finally made his way home. By then six years had passed.

"What happened then?"

Miss Larch was scanning the marriage and birth records. "He married a local girl and they had a son, but it seems he never left the house once he came back home to Sidwell. His wife did all the business. No one ever really saw him again." She turned a few of the old, crinkly pages. "There was obviously something or someone who mattered to him at Mourning Dove Cottage."

In his will, he'd left a sum for upkeep that paid the taxes for the cottage through all the years it was abandoned.

"I suspect he wanted to keep it up in case the previous occupant ever returned," Miss Larch said.

The memory tea we were drinking was definitely working, because I remembered something personal. Something I hadn't thought about for a long time. At the end of the summer long ago when I had to give up the part of the witch, I'd found a note left on our porch.

Good-bye had been written in blue ink.

Your friend, Collie

Maybe I'd mattered to somebody, too.

CHAPTER SEVEN

How to Reverse a Curse

When Agate and Julia came back from Brooklyn I was waiting on the front porch of Mourning Dove Cottage. Beau came running over, barking hello, and Dr. and Mrs. Hall both gave me a hug and said it was good to be home. Agate had her hands full with fabric that she'd bought in Manhattan. "Silk, satin, velvet, tweed!" she sang out, racing in to get to work at her sewing machine.

At the library in Brooklyn the sisters had discovered that Agnes Early had lived there, and had been a seamstress in a shop famous for its wedding dresses. Agate had clearly inherited her sewing talents from her. A librarian had helped the girls find a copy of the 1790 census. By scanning through, they had discovered that Agnes had done well enough to buy her own property. Although she had never married, her younger sister Isabelle had. Aggie was devoted to her niece and nephews, one of whom was Julia and Agate's three-times-great-grandfather.

Then it was time for my news. I announced that I knew who was pretending to be the monster.

"You do?" Julia applauded me on what she said was my fine investigative work. "Did you set a trap?"

"I didn't have to. I saw him in the woods. He's just a boy who used to spend summers here when he was little. I think he's trying to protect the owls."

"Well, he's making things worse for your brother." Julia reached for her backpack and took out a flyer that had been left behind the windshield wipers of her father's car that morning.

MONSTER HUNT
It is advised for all townspeople to bring
bats, guns, knives, nets, flashlights, lanterns.
Meet in front of Town Hall at 8 a.m.

A shiver ran through me.

"It's tomorrow morning," Julia told me. "What if they search our houses?"

I couldn't even begin to answer that question. It was too horrible to consider.

If they searched our house, my brother would be found.

It was dusk when James and I walked through the orchard together. We didn't speak as the colors of evening sifted down around us. We knew our lives were about to change. I'd shown him the flyer about the monster hunt. He'd read it, then crumpled it in one hand. I'd never seen his eyes that dark. I picked up the flyer and folded it into my pocket so my mother wouldn't happen upon it.

The garden had grown so tall no one could see us. We met Agate and Julia in the center, where the four paths crossed each other. It was only fitting it should be the four of us. We were in it together and together we could break the spell and stop the monster hunt however we could. Julia was trying her best not to stare at my brother's wings, which were folded on his back. If you didn't look too closely, it appeared that a cape had been thrown over his shoulders.

"We have to end where Aggie began," I said. "That's the only way to reverse the curse."

"It doesn't matter what we do. I'll never be normal." James turned to Agate. "I can't drag you into this."

He stalked out of the garden even though Agate did her best to call him back. He didn't seem to hear her, but she was convinced she could change his mind.

"I'll talk sense into him," she said.

She scrawled a note on a piece of paper and gave it to me to deliver. I went home and ran up to the attic, but James wouldn't answer when I knocked and called his name. He was stubborn. It was his one bad trait. Once his mind was made up, he wouldn't listen. He was like my mother in that way. In the end I slipped the note under his door.

That evening, Agate waited in the meadow, as she'd written she would. All of the fireflies were fading. It grew so late, she fell asleep in the grass. Owls came and went. But James never appeared.

He went out that night. When I looked out my window I noticed his shadow pass over the lawn as he flew north, toward the mountains. I climbed up to the attic, and saw that all the windows had been left open. Flash was gone. It was likely he'd followed James to one of his secret places in the woods, where no one would find him.

I knew that birds belonged in the sky. But my brother belonged with us.

He'd left a last note for me to deliver, so I was the one who met Agate in the meadow just as she was waking up. Her pale hair was loose, her feet were bare. Her black dress was rumpled. The early-morning light was yellow, like a cat's eye, and the air was crackly with heat and humidity, the way it is before a storm. I knew what my brother wrote, because when Agate dropped it on the grass I picked it up and read it. I don't know if that was right or wrong, but once I'd read the note I knew that he didn't wish to hurt her, that he only wanted her happiness, and that he believed she could never find that with the Sidwell Monster. By the time they came hunting for him, he'd be long gone. I walked home through the garden where the spell had been created. Two rose petals were in the path. I picked them up and slipped them into my pocket. I thought they might bring me luck, and I needed good fortune now.

I'd made a mess of things. If I'd never watched the Halls moving in, or climbed the apple tree, or fallen and broken my arm, if I'd never told him about Agate, if he'd never seen her standing in the grass outside our house, if I'd just stayed out of it, James might be safe at home instead of in the woods, all alone.

I had to tell my mother the truth. All those times I'd been late, when I made up excuses, I'd been at Mourning Dove Cottage. I'd wanted a friend so desperately, I had lied, and I'd kept secrets; now because of it, James had disappeared.

We were sitting at the kitchen table. I couldn't even bring myself to look at my mother when I admitted all I'd done. I was ready for her to tell me what a disappointment I was, but instead she took my hand in hers.

"I knew you were going there, Twig. I didn't stop you because I also knew how much you wanted a friend."

My eyes were stinging as I held back tears. "But I was lying to you!"

"Only because the rules were unfair."

When my mother came to hug me, I felt something open inside me, my love for her and my gratitude for all she'd tried to do for us, even if some of it had turned out wrong.

"Let's go find him," she said.

We looked all over town, stopping at the places James told me he'd visited in the dark—the library and Town Hall—but we saw no sign of him. My mother had me go over to the Starline Diner while she searched the side streets. Mr. Rose was at the counter. He had ordered a slice of my mother's Pink peach summer pie.

"Twig," Mr. Rose said when he saw me. "Are you okay?"

I probably looked like I'd been crying. "I'm trying to find someone who doesn't want to be found."

"That can be as hard as looking for a shadow."

I handed Mr. Rose the crumpled-up flyer that I had shoved into my pocket. He nodded, upset.

"My aunt has been worried about the possibility of a monster hunt for some time. As a matter of fact, she called me about this before I got the job at the paper. That's one of the reasons I came. I'm going to see what I can do to stop this nonsense."

Mr. Rose headed to his office, waving to me from the street.

Sally Ann came over, concerned. "Can I get you something, honey?" she asked. "Maybe something for your mom?"

She was so nice, I nodded, and Sally Ann gave me a coffee-to-go for my mother and an oatmeal cookie for me.

"On the house," she told me. "Friends are friends, even when they don't see each other much."

I ran out to our car, where my mother was waiting. "Sally Ann sent you this."

"She always was thoughtful," my mother said.

I handed over the coffee and she took a few sips. Then we drove into the mountains. We parked on the side of the road and made our way through the woods, calling for my brother. We saw a blue heron take flight. We saw deer and raccoon tracks. We saw mice as they darted away from us. But we didn't see any sign of James.

At home, after my mother had gone to her room, where I could hear her crying, I went out to search again by myself. I walked along until I reached the old road where white stones had been scattered. On a rock beside the huge fence surrounding the Montgomery estate, there was a small blue-painted monster. I leaned over and stood on my hands. I was shaky, but I was up long enough to see the owl's face once more. For some reason, that gave me courage.

A few things had fallen out of my pockets, including my house key and some quarters, and I bent to gather all I could see in the shadows. I took a deep breath and went through the old gate, and after that I just kept going. The house loomed in the falling dusk. I rang the bell and stood back. No one answered, but when I turned Colin Montgomery was on the lawn.

"My father is out to dinner," he said. "It's just me."

He looked exactly the same as he had when we were little, only different.

"Collie," I said. "You're the monster."

He nodded, then sat down in the grass. I went to sit beside him. Maybe when you know someone when you're really young, you always feel like you know him.

"It was the only way I could think of to try to stop my father from destroying the woods. This is the only place I've ever felt at home."

"You're not the only person who feels that way."

He nodded. "That's why I've been helping Dr. Shelton."

"You mean stealing for him."

"Borrowing. And leaving signs to convince people to vote against any building in the woods."

"Well, now people in town are going on a monster hunt. That's why my brother disappeared."

"You have a brother?"

I don't know why I trusted him, but I did. Maybe it was because he was the only friend I'd ever had before

I met Julia. Maybe it was because of the note he left me all those years ago. The bond we'd shared fully returned when he explained that he had lost his mother the year we were in summer camp. That's why he'd hated his lunches, because the housekeeper made them, and that's why he was grateful to me for sharing what was mine and homemade.

"James is the monster," I said.

Collie laughed, until he saw my solemn expression.

"There are no monsters," he said back.

"People in Sidwell think there are."

"Then we'll have to change their minds," Collie told me.

It was in the newspaper the following day, taking up the entire front page.

MONSTER COMES FORWARD TO SPEAK

Underneath there was a photograph of Colin Montgomery. He had confessed to being responsible for all of the thefts and graffiti in town. After he'd walked me home, he'd gone to the sheriff's office. His father had arrived and told him not to say a word without a lawyer present, but Collie had told his story to the sheriff and to

Ian Rose and to anyone else who would listen. He had pretended to be the Sidwell Monster to get everyone's attention. "Vote no at the town meeting," he said just before his father called in a lawyer from Boston and paid the fine, so that he was let go.

I wanted to thank Collie. I knew he'd confessed because of James, and maybe, just a little, because of me. I started off toward the Montgomery estate, but when I reached Last Lake I stopped. I had a sinking feeling. I spied Julia and Collie sitting on the dock talking. I heard them laughing. I could just see them from the back, but I didn't have to see more to know what had happened. I ran back the way I had come, my face hot.

I should have expected as much. I was Twig, the invisible. Twig, whom no one really noticed. It made sense to me that they would like each other more than they liked me. I cried as I ran, but by the time I went through the orchard my tears were gone and I felt cold.

I'd lived my whole life without a friend. I'd just have to remember how to do that again.

Even though I wouldn't have to lie to my mother any-more, I didn't go over to Mourning Dove. Without James, our house was quieter, and I wanted it that way. When Julia called, I didn't answer the phone. What was there to say? That we'd been friends, but that I didn't trust her anymore? That we'd almost reversed the curse? Sometimes I would spy Agate standing outside our house in the dark. She came when she thought no one would see her, but I always did, maybe because we were both scanning the sky for James. She resembled a ghost, with her knotted hair and chalky complexion. Now I under-stood my mother's wish. I wished we could go backward in time to the beginning of the summer, when every-thing was different, and all things seemed possible.

On the morning of August 1, a hot, blue Saturday, when the whole town was getting ready to attend the play at Town Hall, Julia appeared at our back door. She didn't even knock, she just walked inside, even though she'd never been there before. I was washing the dishes, and I was so startled, I dropped a glass. It shattered in the sink. The truth was, other than James, the person I missed most was Julia. I forgot that the water in the sink was running. I forgot about the broken glass.

"I know you don't want to talk to me because James ran away and you probably blame us." She seemed sad, but also sure of herself. She came over and shut off the running water. "Even if you don't want to be friends anymore, I do."

"Do you?" I said. "Don't you have another friend you'd rather be with?"

Julia furrowed her brow, confused.

"I saw you with Colin at the lake."

Julia laughed. "That's what you're upset about?" She took out an envelope. "He was leaving this for you. I said I'd take it to you, but every time I called to come over, you wouldn't answer. He said you'd dropped this near his house, and he thought it would bring you luck. He told me he never had a better friend in Sidwell than you've been to him. When he asked if I would mind sharing you I said I would be perfectly happy to."

I folded the envelope into my pocket, and then I threw my arms around Julia. I had missed her so much.

"Perfect," I said.

"And there's more," Julia said. "I think I found something important."

She placed a sheet of very old paper on our kitchen table. The edges were crumbling and the ink was faint. "It fell out of the drawer when my mother took the desk to the antique store. It's the last page of Agnes's diary. It must have been torn out."

The recipe for the spell.

Take every herb in the garden in equal measure, a teaspoon of each, and add two petals of the most beautiful flower of all. Stand in the center of the garden on the night of the Red Moon. Burn the herbs and let the smoke rise upward.

Twice say "Fly from me," and mean it from your heart.

Julia said she had looked up the phases of the moon in the *Sidwell Herald*.

The Red Moon was the first full moon in August.

"It's two nights from now," Julia said. "August third."

We still had time after all.

We went to work in the Halls' garden, picking the herbs and drying them in the sun. We worked all day. The weather was so hot we used big oak leaves to fan ourselves, but we knew we couldn't stop until we'd gathered all of our ingredients.

We were just about to look at Agnes's recipe and make sure we had every element we needed when Mrs. Hall came looking for us. She came hurrying through the mint, a worried expression on her face. "Have you seen Agate?" she asked. "She said she would come home and take a nap, and then we'd go to the play together."

The scent of herbs rose into the air; it smelled like the tea my mother drank on winter nights. It was dusk and most people were on their way to Town Hall to see *The Witch of Sidwell* at the summer festival. I certainly didn't plan on going.

"I saw her this morning," Julia said. "When she left for Town Hall."

"I just looked for her in her room." Mrs. Hall's face was grim. "I don't know where she went. All I know is that her suitcase is gone."

CHAPTER EIGHT

A Sky Filled with Lightning

I JUMPED INTO THE CAR WHEN DR. HALL called out, gesturing for everyone to get in. We drove to Main Street in complete silence, all of us worried for Agate.

Evening had fallen and the weather had changed suddenly, as it sometimes does in the summertime in our part of Massachusetts. One minute it's hot and sunny, and the next you're shivering. A storm was blowing in from the east with banks of inky dark clouds. We could hear thunder echoing over the mountains as the sky turned even darker. All the birds were hiding in their nests. Not a single sparrow flitted across the sky. The wind whipped through tree branches, and leaves started to fall and carpet the road. It didn't even seem like summer anymore.

I wondered if my brother was somewhere safe.

I kept the envelope from Collie with me at all times. I would wait for a special time to open it. Until then I really did wish and hope it would bring me luck.

In the gloomy dusk everything in Sidwell looked shadowy and strange. The thunder was constant now. Gusts of wind followed us through the door and people shivered and said we were surely in for terrible weather. They talked about storms of the past, floods and blizzards that had cut Sidwell off from the rest of the world. They remembered that during one summer thunderstorm, lightning had set half the town on fire. I realized that was when the old *Herald* building had burned down and all the files were lost.

By the time we arrived, Town Hall was already jampacked with people, all excited for the play to begin. Before it could, Hugh Montgomery jumped onto the stage and took the microphone.

"Hello, everyone," he said. "I know you've been reading some negative things about my family in the *Herald*, but I hope you will vote yes at the next town meeting and allow Sidwell to move into the future."

I saw Colin sitting in the back row by himself. He waved when he saw me and I waved back. I thought how lonely he must have been at the estate all those summers, almost as lonely as James, as lonely as I'd been.

"Your future, not ours," Mr. Hopper from the garden center shouted back from the audience. "What would Sidwell be without the woods? Just another slab of asphalt filled with stores that nobody needs."

While the mayor took the microphone to suggest that the place for this discussion was the town meeting, we went backstage. The kindergartners were all in costume. I noticed the vests Agate had sewn. Just seeing them made me feel sad. She had put so much work into each one.

Mrs. Meyers, the drama teacher, was going over lines with the little witch. When she noticed us poking around, she came over. Only the cast and crew were allowed backstage.

"You should be in the audience," Mrs. Meyers told us. "We're almost ready to begin."

The thunder was closer now. When a boom rumbled right over our heads, the girl playing the little witch jumped. Her costume was the best, just as Agate had said it would be, with a pretty lace collar and a black skirt that looked like a silk waterfall. The girl was the granddaughter of Mr. Hopper. I'd seen him sitting proudly in the first row when we passed by on our way backstage. "The little witch is ours," he'd been telling everyone in the audience.

"Was Agate here today?" Dr. Hall asked the drama teacher.

"Of course," Mrs. Meyers said. "She's in charge of costumes. We really couldn't do without her. We'd be utterly lost. She's been such an asset." But Agate was now nowhere to be seen and she didn't answer when Mrs. Meyers called out her name. "That's odd," the drama teacher murmured. "She was here a minute ago."

The room was bustling with children and parents. People were hugging, wishing each other well, and making little jokes about the end of the play, when the witch is pushed off the cliff. My least favorite part. "Watch out for falling witches," people advised each other. "What was the witch's favorite subject in school?" I heard someone say. The whole crowd shouted back an answer: "Spelling."

"Agate!" Mrs. Meyers called out, more loudly. She'd been on Broadway long ago and her voice was commanding. Everyone else grew quiet. There was a huge clap of thunder, the loudest and closest yet. This time we all nearly jumped out of our shoes.

"Agate, where are you?" Mrs. Hall shouted, her voice breaking a little.

"I'm sure she's here somewhere," Dr. Hall said in a reassuring way. He had spoken to me in the same comforting manner when I'd fallen out of the tree. He took his wife's arm and led her toward the auditorium. "She wouldn't miss the show."

They were so new to town they had never heard of the play's traditional subject matter. I didn't think they'd really enjoy a play in which a member of their family was denounced as a witch, but they went to take their seats. I sneaked a peek through the velvet curtains. The Halls looked nervous, and Mrs. Hall turned round to search for Agate without the slightest bit of luck.

I was stunned to see that my mother had arrived. She was being guided down the aisle by Mr. Rose. I'd forgotten about dinner and hadn't been home all day. My mother must have thought I'd disappeared, just like Agate.

I wanted to race over to explain that I was fine, but

Julia was signaling frantically from the dressing room. I made my way through a line of children ready to go onstage. They were getting a last-minute pep talk from Mrs. Meyers. "If you forget a line just keep going," she advised. "Don't forget to smile."

Julia and I kept our heads close together so no one would overhear. She had found Agate's suitcase under the makeup counter in the dressing room, and an envelope on which Agate had written: *To my parents and my dear sister Julia.*

"Is it snooping to open it?" Julia asked.

"Your name is on it. She must want you to read it."

The letter smelled a little like Agate's perfume and a little like a garden, a combination of fragrant jasmine and freshly cut grass, possibly because she spent so many hours on our lawn in the dark, waiting for James to come home.

Dear Family,

After the play is over tonight I am taking the bus back to Brooklyn. I wish I could stay in Sidwell, but I have brought grief to a friend here, and I can't stay any longer.

Gone to Brooklyn, just like Agnes Early. It was happening all over again.

"She must have taken off without her suitcase," Julia said.

"Or . . . ," I said.

We exchanged a look.

Or perhaps Agate had hidden when she heard her parents' voices rather than face them and explain all that had happened.

Maybe she was still here.

We knew the play would soon begin, but instead of taking our seats in the auditorium, Julia and I began to search backstage. There were closets, dressing rooms, a cellar, staircases, an attic, and, three stories above us, the bell tower.

By this time the thunder was so close it shook the building. We could hear some of the children out on the stage gasp and cry out for their mothers. "There, there," people in the audience called. "All's well that ends well," a good-natured theatergoer shouted. Lightning had begun to crackle, so close it lit up the sky as if it were daylight.

Julia and I went down to the old stone cellar, figuring we should get the scariest part over first. While we searched for Agate, there was a huge flash of lightning. It sounded like a thousand windows breaking, and the sky lit up as if a million lightbulbs had gone off all at once. Even the cellar windows shimmered white. Quite suddenly the lights went out, not just in Town Hall, but all over Sidwell, as if some giant hand had turned off all the switches, and here we were with no electricity, stuck in the cellar, in the dark. We blinked and held our breath. Then we heard the whoosh of fire above us, on the roof.

Julia and I could hear people shouting upstairs as they searched for their children, and the calm voice of Mrs. Meyers calling: "File out in a single line. Keep calm! Exit at the rear!"

A flash of light came down the stairs, and we blinked in the sudden illumination.

"Hurry," someone called.

We made our way upstairs, stumbling a bit, guiding our steps by keeping our hands on the wall made of rough stones. There was a strange burning odor. Through the windows we could see sparks sifting into the night. Lightning had hit the roof and set it on fire. Flames were pouring out from the bell tower.

Collie was waiting for us at the top of the stairs.

"Let's go," he urged. "This whole place could go up in flames."

Julia refused to go out the emergency exit behind the dressing rooms. "My sister might be trapped!"

As we pleaded with her, Dr. and Mrs. Hall came through the dark. "There you are!" Mrs. Hall grabbed Julia and hugged her tightly. I heard a sob escape from her throat. "We thought we'd lost you, too!"

My mother and Mr. Rose were right behind them, equally frantic. "Teresa Jane!" my mother said. "You know you're not allowed to come to this event! We've been looking everywhere for you!"

"We?" I said.

"I'm a concerned party," Mr. Rose said. "Why wouldn't I be?"

The call of sirens cut through the dark. All three of the town's fire trucks raced up and we could hear their engines rumbling. Sheriff Jackson came through the backstage area with a huge flashlight that he shone in our direction. Everything looked bright and harsh.

"This is an emergency evacuation," he shouted. "You need to be out this minute. Pronto!"

"But—" Dr. Hall began.

"No buts. This building is on fire. Exit now!"

"You don't understand," Dr. Hall insisted. "Our daughter may be in there."

"Do you have any proof?" the sheriff asked. "If not, I can't risk anyone's life."

We were led out onto the street, where crowds of

people watched the roof burn and the firemen did their best to keep it under control. Flashes of lightning continued, so that the sky seemed black and then, suddenly, a bright, blinding white. We shivered in the glare. Collie stood right next to me. Without my saying a word, he knew how frightened I was.

Julia turned to her parents. "We can't just wait here! Agate's suitcase was inside. She was planning on going back to Brooklyn. But we don't know if she really did, or if she's hiding somewhere."

Smoke was streaming all over town, out past the mountains. So many sparks were flying through the air, the sheriff made us all stand in the middle of the town green, far enough away from the fire. Mr. Montgomery came running, frantic, searching for Collie. No matter how they disagreed, they were still father and son. They shook hands, and then Mr. Montgomery threw his arms around Collie.

I heard a shift in the wind. I gazed up and couldn't tell the difference between the stars and the flames. Then my eyes focused and I saw Agate in the bell tower. My heart went crazy. I grabbed Julia's arm. She turned and gasped. Agate had climbed away from the flames on the roof on the ladder that circled around the bell tower. The shaky iron stairs were only used twice a year, when a watchman needed to set the chimes to the correct time.

Dr. and Mrs. Hall clutched on to each other, in shock to see their daughter in the rickety bell tower. Agate stood still, her hair shining, like a star in the sky. There were flames above her and below her. I overheard the firemen say there was no ladder that would reach high enough. I couldn't believe their words. Smoke was billowing into the sky, so thick it seemed we lived in the clouds.

That was when I saw him.

James came from the north, from the mountains. Later he told me he'd spent the past nights in a tree, along with a nest of owls. He'd seen sparks in the air above Sidwell, and he'd followed the foul trail of smoke, worried for the town, and for us, and now, most of all, for Agate. Lightning split the sky again as my brother's shadow fell over Main Street. Some people gasped and others just blinked. At last they were seeing the Sidwell Monster, but unlike the beastly creature they had always imagined, he was only a boy.

"That's your brother?" Collie said.

I nodded. "James."

He flew directly to the bell tower and lifted Agate off her unstable perch. His wings shimmered blue and black and feathers fell as he flew her away from the flames. By now everyone in the street was in shock. The thunder had stopped and there was a hush.

And then there wasn't.

Out of the silence there came the sound of someone clapping. I looked over and saw Mr. Rose, clapping and whooping out with joy. Before long everyone joined in. The whole town went wild with gratitude, the applause like a wave that was louder than thunder.

My brother could have escaped into the woods, where no one would have found him, but instead he landed on Main Street, depositing Agate safely on the pavement. When he set her down, she threw her arms around him.

Flash had followed my brother and now perched in the tree directly above us. The fire was still burning out of control. My brother stared intently at the crowd, uncertain as to how they would react to him. When no one came after him, James must have decided it was safe to finish the job. He grabbed the nearest fire hose and took off into the sky once more. As we watched he put out the fire that most certainly would have destroyed most of Sidwell, as fire had done once before. Now the only thing that had been destroyed was the wooden bell tower.

When James came back to earth, there was silence. And then one of the men from the Gossip Group started to applaud. It may have been Mr. Stern, or one of the others, but soon enough they all joined in. The rest of the town gave a great cheer, and then the residents of Sidwell rushed to my brother, not to arrest him but to celebrate him. They lifted him into the air and paraded him down Main Street. The band that was to perform the music between the acts of *The Witch of Sidwell* instead played "Amazing Grace" and "For He's a Jolly Good Fellow." The little witch who was Mr. Hopper's granddaughter threw out handfuls of fairy dust, which was really a mixture of baking flour and red chalk.

Dr. and Mrs. Hall ran to hug Agate, and when James was let down after being carried along Main Street, they hugged him as well. I saw my mother on a corner, crying, her eyes filled with pride, and Mr. Rose had his arm around her. Collie and Julia stood on either side of me, my two best friends.

I could not believe how perfect this terrible night had become.

The bell tower of Town Hall had to be replaced, but the bell itself was as good as new. If anything it rang more clearly. People said that on Sundays you could hear it all the way in Boston. There was an article in the *Sidwell Herald* the next day about the fire, but there was no mention of a boy with wings, only that James Fowler, a resident of Old Mountain Road, had been the hero of the evening, rescuing Miss Agate Early Hall and saving a Sidwell treasure—the bell that, as it turned out, Miss Larch had discovered had been commissioned by our ancestor Lowell Fowler after the Revolutionary War to ring every evening at the hour when he was to have met his beloved beside Last Lake.

I didn't attend the town meeting where the fate of the woods was decided, but I learned about what had happened in the *Sidwell Herald*. Collie and I sat on my porch steps and read about it together before he had to go back to Boston. There was a photograph of all the citizens of Sidwell who had worked to stop the destruction of the woods, along with Dr. Shelton, whose report had convinced the town council that the breeding ground of the black saw-whet owls must be preserved at all costs. Instead of pitching a fit and bringing in his lawyers, Hugh Montgomery agreed to donate the Montgomery Woods to the town to forever be open land. He would keep only his house, for he planned to spend summers here from now on. It was his son's favorite place in the world, the place where they could be a family.

Julia came over with Beau.

"Collie," she said, "meet Collie."

Beau offered his paw.

"Perfect dog," Collie said.

Julia and I laughed, but we kept the joke to ourselves. Some things you just don't share.

We had the first apple pie of the season, made with tart green apples with honey added, to make sure it was sweet enough. We sat around the kitchen table, three friends who wouldn't see each other until Julia and I convinced our mothers to take us to Boston for a weekend in the fall. We had it all planned out: We'd go to the aquarium, and walk along the Charles River, and visit Concord, where Lowell Fowler had fought in battle, and we'd most definitely have tea in Collie's house on Beacon Hill, black orchid tea, which was still my favorite.

Collie said it was his favorite, too. When we finished our tea, and Julia had gone home, I brought him to Miss Larch's. That was something just the two of us did together on his last day in Sidwell. On the way over he asked if I'd ever gotten the envelope he sent me. I admitted I was saving it, to open after he'd gone back to Boston so I could feel like he was still in Sidwell. "Oh, I'll be back," he told me. "My father and I will be here at Thanksgiving." It was the perfect time of year to get together, the season when we made not only apple pies, but also the once-a-year Pink pumpkin pie that was a great favorite in town.

We met with Miss Larch and Dr. Shelton so that the ornithologist could thank Collie on behalf of the Sidwell owls. He gave Collie a book he'd written about owls. Miss Larch surprised me by giving me a gift as well, her own copy of Emily Dickinson's poems. Whenever I read them I would remember that day, when we drank black orchid tea. In all my years in Sidwell, I think it was the least lonely I'd ever felt.

Not long afterward the mayor came to our door. He was accompanied by Miss Larch, because she was the official town historian and was always interested in matters concerning Sidwell. Mr. Rose came as well. He had a broad grin on his face and I could tell he was there not as a journalist, but because of his interest in our family. James was there, too, and that was very exciting. He had moved out of the attic, and now had the bedroom next to mine.

"No more hiding," my mother had said. "We are who we are."

As it turned out, everyone in Sidwell agreed. A second vote had been taken at the town meeting after the Montgomery land development had been defeated, and once again the results were unanimous. It was decided that what had happened in Sidwell would remain in the Sidwell archives. What really transpired on the night of the fire would be kept secret, a story Sidwell residents would cherish and tell only to their daughters and sons. All of the T-shirts with images of the Sidwell Monster had been burned in a bonfire. The mayor had Miss Larch take a photograph of him shaking James's hand for the files in the history room.

Mr. Rose stayed on when the mayor left to drive Miss Larch home. We all had glasses of cold Pink apple lemonade. "I could not be more proud of you, James," Mr. Rose said. He then grinned at me. "Or you, Twig." He looked at my mother with a strong expression. "It's about time I met my son and daughter properly."

I think I'd known the truth for some time. He had the same gray-green eyes as James, and the same tall awkwardness that I had. I hadn't shut the door on him the first time he came to our house. I'd wanted to know him.

I wanted to know him now.

When he hugged me I understood what I'd been missing for so long because I wasn't missing it anymore.

We sat on the porch steps and my mother explained why we had left our father behind when we left New York. She hadn't thought it was right to subject him to the sort of future we would have because of James's wings, the secrets that would surround our lives. Just because he'd married into the Fowler family, he didn't have to share our burden and keep secrets. Our father was such an honest man, after all, she didn't want to put him in the position of having to lie every day. She also feared his honesty would make him slip and she just couldn't risk James being found out. She convinced him in her letter that he would endanger James, and that was the last thing he wanted to do.

Our father had respected her wishes, even though he'd been missing us all that time. Miss Larch had sent him photos of me that she'd taken at school events. She announced that she was our great-aunt, and that made sense. Thinking back on it, I remembered her at every concert and science fair. She'd always said, "Well, hello, Twig!" as if she were surprised to see me, but now I realized she'd been looking for me in order to keep my father posted, which she always did.

Then Miss Larch had called him in the spring, worried, after hearing about the proposed monster hunt. She thought he should know what his family was up against when it dawned on her that perhaps our mother needed him more than she'd ever admit. That's when he knew he couldn't stay away any longer. That same day he applied for the job at the newspaper.

"Now that we're back together," Mr. Rose said, "my suggestion is that we stay that way."

James grinned and shook our father's hand. I think I might have cried, but only for a moment. I had realized that my name would now be Teresa Jane Rose, and frankly I couldn't have been happier.

CHAPTER NINE

The Night of the Red Moon

ALL FOUR OF US CLIMBED OUT OUR WINDOWS at exactly the same time. It was the one night when the curse could be broken. If we failed, we would have to wait until the following year. By then the curse might be too strong and we'd never get rid of it. There wasn't a single cloud, only handfuls of stars strewn across the darkness and, rising high above us, a huge full moon that seemed red as a rose.

We sat at the corners where the four paths met, right in the middle of the garden we had worked so hard to create all summer long. The air was misty around us and the color and scent of living things surrounded us, black-green mint, tall, plumy grass, wild purple asters. Julia had kept the dried herbs in a leather pouch, and now she placed them into the mixing bowl Mrs. Hall had found in the tangled web of the old garden, back when it was nothing but weeds. We thought the bowl had once belonged to Agnes Early; at least, we hoped it had. When we used it, it seemed that Aggie was with us in some way, and was also on our side. Maybe any powers that she'd once had would help us somehow.

It was a good thing we'd already picked the herbs. It was late in the season and the leaves were wilted from the heat and sunlight. Some of the plants were no longer flowering, including the roses, which had already bloomed and faded. But we were here, and the garden was here, and we had the best intentions, which always matters in magic. We wanted to make things right, the way they had been two hundred years ago before Lowell Fowler disappeared.

It was time to end the curse the way it had begun.

Agate's hair had been singed in the fire and she'd cut it short, using a pair of nail scissors she borrowed from me. If anything she was even more lovely because now you could see her features more clearly. On this night she wore a white dress trimmed with blue ribbon, which she had sewn herself. She was gazing at James, who had a serious, thoughtful expression. He seemed wary and didn't say much. He was with us, but he also seemed alone. I would have guessed he'd be overjoyed that the time to reverse the spell had come. If everything worked as it should, he would soon be free of his wings. I wondered if they would drop off feather by feather, or all at once. Would the process be painful, or would he feel much freer and lighter without the burden of his wings?

We built a small fire out of twigs in the center of the circle. It burned orange and a bright blue and let off little crackling sounds. Just as Julia was about to place the mixing bowl atop the flames, she checked to make certain all of the ingredients had been added. Tansy, mint, lavender, feverfew. She checked once, and then twice, and then she turned pale. One ingredient was missing. No rose petals had been added and now there were none to be had. We didn't realize that the blooms had faded, then had blown away in the storm. I felt as if we'd lost everything, all at once.

"It's my fault," Julia said. "I should have checked."

"Maybe it wasn't meant to happen," James said. "The truth is, I'd miss flying. With wings or without, I lose either way. It's selfish, I know; I just wish I could have it all."

That was when I remembered that I still had the envelope Collie had sent me. I carried it every day for luck, but I'd forgotten to open it. If there was any time I needed luck it was now. Inside were two rose petals. The ones that had fallen from the rosebush in Agnes Early's garden. They'd fallen out of my pocket when I did a handstand near the Montgomerys' gate. It did feel like Collie was still here with us. The petals had turned as dry as paper, but I didn't think that would matter. As my father had told me when he'd first come to our door: *A rose is a rose is a rose.*

Spells are funny things. My brother wanted his life on earth and his life in the air. I wondered if we halved the ingredients, we might have half the cure.

"Maybe you can have what you wish for," I said.

The others looked at me, confused. For once I was the one who was sure of myself. I didn't feel invisible or stupid and I wasn't afraid to say what I thought. I was Teresa Rose, not Twig anymore. I could feel that something inside me had changed. Twig was a girl who spent her time alone and wore her loneliness as if it were armor. For the first time I had everything I wanted, including a family and friends.

I held out the rose petals. "Agnes Early used two. We'll change that. We'll use one. Half the magic."

"What then?" James said, unconvinced. "I'll have one wing?"

"Trust me," I said. It was the only chance that he might get everything he'd ever wanted, his heart's desire, the air and the earth combined.

"I trust you." James went to stand in the north corner.

Agate went to the south corner. Julia and I were at east and west.

Julia peered at Agnes Early's spell. "She said to say 'Fly from me' two times."

"Then we'll say 'Come back to me,'" I said, reversing the curse. "But only once."

"And we'll mean it from our hearts," Agate said.

"And what will happen will happen," James said, his eyes clear and green. "And I'll accept whatever that is."

Julia placed the bowl onto the fire. A pale curl of smoke arose from the herbs as they heated up. I leaned over and added a single rose petal. The smoke turned red and then pink and then a pearly white. We held hands. I don't know about the others but I, for one, closed my eyes.

Come back to me.

We said it together, as if we had one voice, and maybe we did at the moment.

I heard the wind. It whirled around us. A few

raindrops spattered the ground as the gusts blew past us. I kept my eyes closed. I could feel the magic everywhere, in the earth and the sky and in us. It felt like the past and the future braided together, as if our destiny was changing.

Yet when I opened my eyes, nothing had changed. There were still the four of us. Still Agnes Early's garden. Still the Red Moon. Still wings on my brother's back.

We were exhausted and confused. We'd tried everything and it appeared we had failed. Out of respect for the magic of the garden we didn't complain or blame anything or anyone. There wasn't anything left to do but say good night. I think Agate had tears in her eyes when we left each other. Maybe we all did.

James and I hurried home through the orchard. He could have flown, but instead he walked beside me. The trees were filled with leaves and tiny green apples that would turn pink in time.

James threw an arm around my shoulders. "You tried. That's all you can do."

"I wanted to do more than try."

"You did. You showed me how much you care about me."

I wanted to cry for real now, just sob so loudly all the nesting birds would fly away in a cloud. But I didn't.

I was Teresa Jane Rose and I still had faith that every curse could be undone and that somehow there had been magic in the garden.

When I slept that night I dreamed of Agnes Early and of Lowell Fowler and of a moon that was red as a rose. I dreamed I walked through Sidwell in the dark and saw all of our neighbors sleeping, and despite everything that had happened I was glad to live in a town where anything could happen and magic was always a possibility.

In the morning there was the sound of shouting. I recognized James's voice even in my dream.

I'd overslept and now I ran to my brother's room. James was standing there, an amazed expression on his face. His arms were raised, and he was surrounded by a circle of blue-black feathers. They were falling down like the leaves from the trees in autumn.

"It's happening," James said, his voice hoarse.

His wings were folding in upon themselves, as if they had been made of paper. They dropped onto the floor and turned into dust. With one gust of wind through the open window the dust rose into a circle of ash and flew out the window. I felt the same shivery feeling I'd had in the garden, but this time I didn't close my eyes.

And there was James. An ordinary boy.

My brother peered at his reflection in the mirror on the wall.

"I'm like anyone else," he said.

I couldn't tell if he was happy or sad.

"It was just half the cure," I assured him. "You'll have your wings again."

"I doubt that." He shook his head. "What's gone is gone."

He'd been who he was for so long, maybe he feared he wouldn't know how to be ordinary. I'd felt the same way before this summer, and now I was a girl with friends and a family and hope.

"You'll see," I said. "You'll have what you wished for."

Outside the window, the birds James had raised and nursed back to health tapped at the glass. He had had friends, I realized, and a whole world shared with them, one he didn't want to give up.

I found my mother in the kitchen and told her what had happened.

"We tried so hard to let him be like everyone else," I said.

"But he's not like everyone else," my mother said. "He's one of a kind. And that is nothing to be ashamed of."

She telephoned our father, who came as soon as he could. It felt so good to be waiting for him on the front porch, and even better when he threw his arms around me and said, "We'll make it right, Twig. You wait and see."

He went inside and knocked on my brother's door. "Just give me five minutes," he called. He must have had just the right tone, because my brother let him in.

My mother and I waited in the kitchen. Finally, our father came to have a cup of coffee.

"He's thinking things over," our dad said. "It's part of growing up. As life goes on you lose some things and you gain some things. It's true for everyone. James is just facing this all at once."

James thought things over for a long time. Then he came out to have dinner with us. My mother made a tomato corn pie for supper and a peach pie for dessert, with some of the apple cinnamon ice cream our dad had brought. I loved even thinking the word *dad* and I loved that he seemed to know us, even though we'd been separated for so long. And then my mother told us that for all these years they had been writing to each other, and that she'd gotten a post office box and kept all of his letters in a box tied with ribbon under her bed. For all these years she'd been sending him photographs and telling him about our lives, so in a way he really had known us even though we'd been apart. Maybe he hadn't guessed my favorite flavor of ice cream. And maybe he also knew how much we had missed him.

Every bit of our dinner together was delicious. In fact, I think it was the best meal I'd ever had. If we had been in Brooklyn, people would have lined up around the block to buy a single slice of my mother's pie, but because we were in Sidwell, we just ate the whole thing ourselves.

We sat at the table for a long time, telling stories, remembering the fire. The truth was we felt like a family. We had ups and downs, but we were all together.

As the sun was sinking, we went out to the porch. Blackbirds flew over our house and disappeared into the orchard. It was the end of the summer, and we felt it in the air, like a cloak falling over us. There was a single star in the sky, brighter than any I'd spied before.

"I believe that's Venus," our dad said. "You can see it much more clearly here in Sidwell than you can in New York City."

That was when it happened. Magic always sneaks up on you that way, when you least expect it, when the time is absolutely right.

James doubled over and gasped. My mother stood up, ready to run to him, but my father held her back.

"What's meant to be will happen," he told her. They looked at each other so deeply that I realized they'd been together in some way even though they'd been apart for so many years.

We waited together. As darkness fell James's wings grew back, as if they'd never disappeared. He closed his eyes tightly, expecting pain, but later he explained it seemed perfectly natural. It was just the way the petals of night-blooming jasmine, which close up during the day, unfold when the moon is in the sky.

Just as I'd hoped. Half the cure. Half the curse. Half the magic.

There he was, James Fowler Rose, my brother.

"Absolutely perfect," I said.

This year my brother is at school, a senior. He walks Agate to school every day as Julia and I race out in front of them. But at night, he still has his own world. His wings appear as he stands on the roof and all the birds he's ever saved wait for him and follow him into the woods.

School is better than it ever was before. I can just be myself, and be as friendly as I want to be. There's a whole group of girls who are much nicer than I thought they were, and I imagine I'll be going to the Sidwell cinema with them, but for now Julia and I are busy on the weekends. I'm rewriting the play about Agnes Early, with Mrs. Meyers's approval. Julia and I act it out together, playing all the parts. Miss Larch is our audience. We visit her on Sunday afternoons and read bits and pieces to her, and she always applauds and tells us how much better than the original it is. After my father moved in with us on Old Mountain Road, I was afraid that Miss Larch might be lonely, but Dr. Shelton is renting her spare room. They have tea together every day and sometimes Julia and I join them. Black orchid is still my favorite.

The witch is not bad anymore, not the way I've written her, only misunderstood, and very much in love. She doesn't dress in black, but instead she wears a white dress trimmed with blue ribbons, which Agate has sewn. It is so beautiful all the little girls in town want to play the part of the witch and wear that dress. The way we've written it, in the second act, she ends the curse and wishes happiness for the citizens of Sidwell.

I mailed the finished pages to Boston for Collie to read. He was my first friend, after all, and I value his opinion. He told me he thinks I won't have a problem with my wish, and that someday we'll sit in the audience of a

Broadway theater together to watch a play I've written. Because I love Sidwell, I'm not rushing toward my future, but it's nice to know that it's out there, waiting for me.

In front of Town Hall, there is a statue of the local hero who saved our town, a handsome boy of seventeen who wears a cloak that flows to the ground. Very often a small black owl sits on the statue's shoulder, peering down at our town with bright yellow eyes. People say if he flashes his stare at you he'll bring you luck. Tourists like to be photographed beside the statue, especially during the apple festival. They stop in at the tourist center to pick up maps and a copy of the *Sidwell Herald*. They come to walk in our woods, and buy our Pink apple cider, and have Pink apple pie at the Starline Diner. When they picnic on the town green near the statue of our hero, they don't notice what local people know: Under the cloak there are feathers carved into the stone. Aside from that, our hero looks like an ordinary boy and in many ways, he is. Now if anyone sees him up above us on nights when there is a full moon, they simply wave and go about their business, grateful to live in a town like Sidwell, a place where the apples are always sweet and mysterious creatures are always welcome.

Pink Apple Pie

*The wonderful baker Mary Flanagan helped me to create a lovely
pink apple pie with two different toppings, including a crumble-top
variation. Best if shared with a friend. But isn't everything?*

PASTRY INGREDIENTS
1-1/2 cups flour
3/4 cup butter
1/4 cup sugar
4-1/2 tablespoons cold water

*You can also use two premade 9-inch crusts bought at the market.
Or see below for crumble-top variation.**

FILLING INGREDIENTS
6 to 8 medium apples
1 cup seedless strawberry jam
3 tablespoons seedless raspberry jam

MAKING THE PASTRY
Preheat oven to 375°F. Butter a nine-inch pie plate.

Sift flour into bowl. Mix in butter (with your fingers!),
smooshing it into flour. Add sugar and mix. Add cold water
a little at a time (you may not need it all). Mix until it forms
a dough.

Wrap dough in plastic wrap and chill in fridge for 20 minutes.

Remove dough from refrigerator. Let stand at room temperature for a few minutes if necessary until slightly softened.

Divide pastry into two balls and roll out with rolling pin. Put one crust into pie plate and form to the plate's size. Save the second crust for the top of the pie.

MAKING THE FILLING

Peel, core, and slice apples. Mix in strawberry jam and place the apple/jam mixture in pastry in pie plate. Dollop with spoonfuls of raspberry jam.

Cover apple mixture with second pastry crust. Pinch crusts together with wet fingers around the sides.

Pierce top of pie with fork (you can make a design if you'd like) to release air as it bakes.

Bake for approximately 40 minutes at 375°F.

*VARIATION: CRUMBLE TOPPING

If using this topping, make half the pastry recipe above (3/4 cup flour, 6 tablespoons butter, 2 tablespoons sugar, 2-1/4 tablespoons cold water). This will make one crust. Fill the crust as above, then add topping.

1 cup flour
1/2 cup butter, at room temperature
1/2 cup sugar

Mix the flour with cut-up butter (with your fingers!) until it forms crumbs. Add sugar and mix. Sprinkle on top of pie.

Bake for approximately 40 minutes at 375°F.

Acknowledgments

With extreme gratitude to the three people who believed in Nightbird and Twig from the start:

My beloved publisher, Barbara Marcus
My brilliant editor, Wendy Lamb
My wonderful agent, Tina Wexler

Many thanks also to the stellar art team at Random House: Isabel Warren-Lynch, Kate Gartner, and Trish Parcell. And thank you to Tracy Heydweiller in production and Tamar Schwartz in managing editorial.

Thanks to Jenny Golub and Colleen Fellingham for their copyediting expertise. Many thanks to Dana Carey for help along the way.

Thank you to the amazing artist Sophie Blackall for her inspiring vision and gorgeous red moon.

Gratitude to my agents, Amanda Urban and Ron Bernstein.

My thanks always to my readers, without whom my books would not come to life.

My deepest gratitude is to Edward Eager, my favorite writer throughout my childhood, whose beautiful books introduced me to magic in the world. I would have been lost without those novels.

About the Author

ALICE HOFFMAN is the author of more than thirty best-selling works of fiction, including *Practical Magic*, also a major motion picture with Sandra Bullock and Nicole Kidman; *Here on Earth*, an Oprah's Book Club selection; the highly praised historical novel *The Dovekeepers*; and, most recently, *The Museum of Extraordinary Things*.

Her books for teens include *Green Angel*, *Green Witch*, *Incantation*, *The Foretelling*, *Indigo*, and *Aquamarine*, also a major motion picture with Emma Roberts.